"They're not going to get away with this. I'm not going to let them."

Every word rang with determination, leaving Elena with no doubt that Matt fully intended to do what he promised.

Them. It didn't matter if it was only one person.

This damn town. She should have gotten out when she'd had the chance, should have left it behind her and never looked back.

Matt gently turned her around to face him. "Don't let them do this to you. You're going to make it through this."

It was the tenderness in his voice more than the words themselves that called to Elena, making her raise her head to meet his eyes.

The kindness she saw there, the concern, nearly broke her. She couldn't even remember the last time anyone had looked at her like that, when anyone had so genuinely cared about her feelings.

Then the look in Matt's eyes changed, became more heated, more intense. And out of nowhere, Elena felt her body respond. The emotions that had been churning within her ebbed away, replaced by an incredible sense of warmth that flowed outward to fill every part of her.

This wasn't nostalgia. This wasn't a remembered emotion. It was real, and it was more powerful than anything she remembered....

KERRY CONNOR

HER COWBOY AVENGER

HARLEQUIN®

entertain, enrich, inspire™

To The Old Book Barn in Forsyth, Illinois, where I first discovered Harlequin Intrigue and so many wonderful books.

Recycling programs
for this product may
not exist in your area.

ISBN-13: 978-0-373-69637-6

HER COWBOY AVENGER

Copyright © 2012 by Kerry Connor

www.Harlequin.com

Printed in U.S.A.

ABOUT THE AUTHOR

A lifelong mystery reader, Kerry Connor first discovered romance suspense by reading Harlequin Intrigue books and is thrilled to be writing for the line. Kerry lives and writes in New York.

Books by Kerry Connor

HARLEQUIN INTRIGUE
1067—STRANGERS IN THE NIGHT
1094—BEAUTIFUL STRANGER
1129—A STRANGER'S BABY
1170—TRUSTING A STRANGER
1207—STRANGER IN A SMALL TOWN
1236—SILENT NIGHT STAKEOUT
1268—CIRCUMSTANTIAL MARRIAGE
1334—HER COWBOY DEFENDER
1370—HER COWBOY AVENGER

Don't miss any of our special offers. Write to us at the following address for information on our newest releases.

Harlequin Reader Service
U.S.: 3010 Walden Ave., P.O. Box 1325, Buffalo, NY 14269
Canadian: P.O. Box 609, Fort Erie, Ont. L2A 5X3

CAST OF CHARACTERS

Elena Weston—Her husband's death turned her into an outcast and a murder suspect—and brought back the one man she never thought she'd see again.

Matt Alvarez—The cowboy came back into her life just when she needed him most.

Bobby Weston—Elena's husband seemed to have no enemies, so why had someone killed him?

Walt Bremer—The sheriff thought he had his killer.

Travis Gerard—The deputy wanted nothing more than to see Elena pay.

Glen Marshall—The family friend offered his help, but how pure were his motives?

Carter Baines—The ranch hand wasn't a fan of Elena.

Jack Landry—The lawyer wanted Elena behind bars.

Lynda Clayton—The woman seemed unusually interested in Matt.

Chapter One

He didn't know what he was doing here.

Matt Alvarez eased his foot off the gas pedal as the sign announcing the town limits of Western Bluff, Texas, appeared up ahead. The truck slowly decelerated, gradually coming to a stop just before the sign.

Welcome to Western Bluff.

It was likely to be the only welcome he received in this town. It hadn't been a particularly friendly place the first time he'd been here, and he wasn't counting on that having changed much. When he'd left eight years ago, no one had bothered telling him goodbye, and he doubted there were many who'd remember him all these years later.

No, there was only one person he could count on remembering him. The person who'd reached out and brought him back after all this time.

From what he could see, the town up ahead looked the same. Short, square buildings were lined up along what passed for a Main Street. Around it stretched the dry desert landscape as far as the eye could see.

It wasn't too late to turn back. It sure as heck would make a lot more sense than driving all the way from New Mexico to this dusty West Texas town in the middle of nowhere, all because of a newspaper article he'd received in the mail.

That article lay heavily in the front pocket of his shirt, tucked in the envelope it had arrived in. He didn't know for sure who'd sent it; there hadn't been a return address. But there was only one person he could imagine sending it. He just couldn't understand why. For help, he supposed. If the story in the article was true, she could probably use it.

That didn't explain why she would have sent it to him of all people, nor why he had come.

He'd been asking himself that last one from the moment he'd climbed into the truck and during every stretch of the drive.

Now he was finally here, and he still didn't have an answer.

Whatever the reason, he couldn't sit there in the middle of the highway forever. The road was clear enough—he didn't see anyone coming up behind him in the rearview mirror—probably not a surprise given the size of the town up ahead. Few people would have a reason to pass through this out-of-the-way place.

But here he was nonetheless.

With a sigh, he moved his foot to the accelerator and put the truck back into motion.

He slowly drove into town, taking in his surroundings as he passed along the main drag. Just as he'd expected, an up-close inspection revealed it really hadn't changed at all. The buildings were all the same, with no signs of any new ones having been built and no alterations on the existing ones as far as he could tell. He still recognized the names of some of the businesses—the lawyer's office, the bank, the Realtor. It was almost as if he'd never left, he realized as an uncomfortable feeling slid down his spine, with the town preserved exactly as it had been the last time he'd been here.

He didn't see many people around, which was kind of odd for two o'clock in the afternoon in any town. But then, it wasn't as though there were that many people in this town to begin with, and he supposed most were at work. There were only a few pedestrians on the sidewalks. He couldn't help but search out the faces of those he did see, even before he realized he was doing it, looking for anyone who appeared familiar.

Or a particular someone, he had to acknowledge, even though the idea gave him no pleasure.

He started to focus back on the road when he caught sight of a dark blue pickup truck up ahead pulling into a parking space on the street. It had barely come to a stop before the driver's-side door opened. A moment later a lean, unmistakably female body emerged, shoulder-length black hair ruffling slightly in the wind.

And there she was.

Damned if his heart didn't stop in his chest, just for an instant.

He hadn't seen her in eight years, a long enough period of time that he shouldn't have been able to recognize her immediately. Eight years was a long time. People changed. But the moment he caught sight of her, he knew it was her.

Elena Reyes—Elena Weston now, evidently.

The only woman he'd ever believed himself in love with.

A woman who—if there was any truth to the newspaper article in his pocket—was now a murderer.

EVEN BEFORE SHE CLIMBED OUT OF the truck, Elena could feel eyes on her. She would have been surprised if it had been any other way—after all, this was her first trip into town in nearly a week—but in this instance she would have loved to be surprised. She resisted the instinctive urge to glance around and see who was watching her, unwilling to let them know she was uncomfortable with their scrutiny.

Let them look. She didn't have anything to be ashamed of. She hadn't done anything wrong.

It took some effort to remember that as she closed the door of the truck and headed to the grocery store, that oppressive feeling of being watched growing in intensity. Luckily, there'd been a parking space close to the entrance so she wouldn't have to walk far, which was the first bit of luck she'd had in weeks. She made herself keep her head high and her shoulders straight as she walked, refusing to do anything that would make it look like she felt guilty.

Still, when she reached the door she paused on the threshold for the briefest of moments and took a deep breath to prepare herself before stepping inside.

As soon as she did, she wasted no time, quickly picking up a basket from inside the door and heading down the nearest aisle. It took less than ten seconds before she felt the air inside the store change, the shift as noticeable as a sudden chill wind blowing in her wake. The light buzz of conversation in the space evaporated, replaced by an eerie stillness that seemed to fill the store.

She wanted to believe it was her imagination. She knew better than to think it was.

She knew how judgmental this town could be, knew what it was like to have people look at her a certain way because of who she was. She'd grown up enduring those looks. But there was a big difference between being the daughter of Ed Reyes, the town drunk, and having everyone believe she'd killed her husband.

As she moved through the aisles, a few people turned rather sharply away as she approached. Several others openly stared. Glared, was more like it. Elena did her best to avoid eye contact. Lord knew she didn't exactly have the energy to deal with outright hostility. Still, she couldn't help but see them out of the corner of her eye and place names to the faces. Connie Raymond, who worked at the local beauty parlor. Delia Hart, whose son had worked for Bobby last summer.

No one said a word to her. No one had to. She knew exactly what they were thinking.

Murderer.

She'd known coming into town would be an ordeal, but there'd been no way around it. She was completely out of supplies, and if she didn't want to starve she was going to have to come and buy groceries. There was no one around to do it for her. The few ranch hands Bobby had still had around had quit, having no interest in working for her, most of them likely knowing she had no way of paying them anyway. Joann Bloom, the cook who'd worked for the Westons for years, had left, as well. She'd said her husband was making her quit, but Elena figured Joann hadn't fought the order too hard, if she had at all. Joann's loyalty had to be with the Westons. Even if Elena could pay her, Joann wouldn't want to keep working for the person accused of killing the last of them.

So it was just Elena, rambling around in the old ranch house with the walls rapidly closing in around her, trying to figure a way out of this mess, wondering what she was going to do. Until the need for supplies had finally forced her into town.

Now though, feeling the stares of half the people around her and the cold shoulders of the others, she couldn't help but wonder if starvation wouldn't have been the better option.

As she rounded the corner to the dairy section, she suddenly found herself facing Cassie Gerard, whose husband, Travis, was Bobby's closest friend—and one of the deputies determined to prove Elena's guilt. Cassie stood in front of the milk cooler, looking toward Elena as if she'd known she was coming.

Their eyes met. Elena froze, uncertain what to say. They'd never exactly been best friends, had only been thrown together because their husbands were, but they'd socialized for years, had dinner at each other's homes, spent holidays together. Yet Cassie stared at her, her expression completely blank, as though she didn't know her at all.

Finally, Elena tried to muster a smile.

Before she could manage it, Cassie turned on her heel and pointedly walked away.

Everything inside Elena deflated like a punctured balloon.

These were people she'd known for years. Her neighbors. They knew her. They knew she wasn't a murderer. At least they should.

But their responses proved they didn't.

Figuring she had enough in her basket to make do for a while, she made her way back to the front of the store. There was no one in line to check out when she got there. Moving to the counter, she quickly unloaded the basket, then set it aside in the stack on the floor.

Only when she straightened did she realize the cashier—Candice Dobson, a local girl Elena had known practically the girl's whole life—hadn't made a move to begin ringing her up. She stood frozen, simply staring at Elena, eyes wide, as if she didn't know what to do.

"Is there a problem?" Elena asked, keeping her tone as pleasant and neutral as possible.

Uncertainty etched across her face, Candice glanced over her shoulder.

Elena followed her gaze. Jacob Higgs, the store manager, stood in the doorway of his office, arms folded over his chest, staring at her.

Finally, he nodded once.

Candice immediately began grabbing Elena's purchases and ringing them up, her motions jerky as she moved as quickly as possible.

Elena never took her eyes from Jacob. She nearly had the ridiculous urge to thank him. But for what? For doing what he was supposed to do and not refusing to serve her? Not to mention, there wasn't the slightest hint of kindness in his hard face as he continued staring at her. Whatever his reasons for not blocking her purchases, it hadn't been to be nice.

Heck, he probably wanted to make sure she didn't drop dead before she could stand trial.

I haven't even been arrested! she wanted to yell, but it was clear she'd be wasting her breath. Nobody here wanted to hear it. They probably thought it was only a matter of time.

It was an opinion she shared much of the time, she acknowledged, her stomach clenching with fear. Sheriff

Bremer had made no secret of the fact he thought she was guilty and was doing everything he could to prove it. The only company she'd had at the house during the past week had been him and his men as they'd searched the house, not bothering to be gentle as they'd tossed all her possessions here and there in an attempt to find evidence. They hadn't, but Elena knew better than to think that would mean they'd stop trying.

Candice finally finished ringing her up. "Twenty-three fifty." She announced the total without looking up, focusing on bagging Elena's purchases. Once she was done, she extended her hand for Elena's money, quickly making change and handing it back to her.

"Thank you," Elena said politely as she accepted it.

Candice didn't say anything, simply lowering her head and not looking at Elena any longer.

Cheeks burning, Elena picked up the two bags and headed to the exit.

Once outside, she began to fumble in her purse for her keys, more than ready to get out of here as quickly as possible. Her attention on juggling the bags in her arms, it wasn't until she was almost to her truck that she noticed something was wrong. The truck was leaning oddly on one side. She glanced down.

The front tire was flat.

No, she realized, her gaze shifting. Both the front and back tires on this side were flat.

She skidded to a stop, clutching the bags in her arms, her heart suddenly pounding in her chest as she came to the inescapable conclusion.

Someone had slashed the tires.

Part of her immediately tried to reject the idea, not

wanting to believe it, not wanting to believe someone she knew could do such a thing.

But it was the only explanation. Two tires on the same side of a truck didn't just go flat on their own. No, this was deliberate. Someone had done this, purposely, maliciously, to hurt her. Someone she knew. A neighbor. Someone she might have once considered a friend.

Tears of frustration suddenly burned the back of her eyes. She did everything she could to hold them at bay, not about to let a single person in this town know they'd driven her to that and grant them the satisfaction. The mere thought of the smug, vengeful expressions that would no doubt greet her tears was enough to make them dry up.

Unable to bear the sight of her flattened tires, she started to back away, only to immediately collide with something. Big hands closed around her upper arms. A man.

Anger surged through her, killing the numbness that had fallen over her. She lunged forward and jerked out of his grip. The cold stares and whispers were bad enough, but damned if she was going to put up with being physically accosted. She whirled around to face her attacker, her mouth opening to tell him exactly what she thought—

The words died, every thought in her head and every trace of anger vanishing as she laid eyes on the man in front of her. She could only stare, unable to fully comprehend what she was seeing.

A single word rose in her mind, like a distant echo spoken by someone else.

Matt.

For an instant, she was twenty again, staring up

into the eyes of the man she loved more than anything she'd ever imagined. The man whose presence sent her heart racing and her stomach clenching whenever he was close. The man who inspired feelings and passions so deep and fierce that everything she'd experienced before that seemed like nothing. The man who filled her thoughts every waking moment and in all of her dreams. The man she didn't believe she would ever be able to live without.

The man who hadn't loved her enough. Or maybe she hadn't loved him enough. She'd spent a great deal of time over the years wondering which it had been. She never had arrived at an answer.

Then she was back in the present. Because the man in front of her wasn't the one she'd loved. This man was older, faint lines worn into the skin around his eyes, his face harder, his body bigger and more muscular. This was Matt Alvarez, with eight more years—years he'd lived without her—on him.

He was still the most beautiful man she'd ever seen. That lustrous black hair, those piercing dark eyes, that magnificent face, somehow even more devastating than the last time she'd seen him.

Of course, the last time she'd seen him she hadn't been looking at his face. She'd been staring at his back as he'd walked away from her.

She'd officially lost her mind. That had to be it. That vaguely unreal feeling she'd been experiencing since Bobby's death, the sense that none of this could be happening, washed over her, stronger than ever. Because there was absolutely no way that Matt Alvarez could be right here, right now.

"Hello, Elena."

And yet he was. Because even eight years later, that voice remained the same.

"Matt" was all she could bring herself to say, her mind still incapable of reconciling the fact that he was actually here in front of her.

"We need to talk."

"About what?" she answered automatically.

"I think you know."

At the moment she was starting to doubt if she knew even her own name. "What are you doing here?"

"That's what we need to talk about." He looked up and glanced around them. "But not here."

Elena repeated his gesture. There were a few people in view on the sidewalk and in nearby vehicles, none of them openly watching her and Matt, though she had no doubt they were. She could only imagine how many others were observing from the windows of the storefronts. Her earlier urge to get out of town and back to the solitude of the ranch as quickly as possible returned with a vengeance. "No," she agreed. "Definitely not here."

"Why don't I give you a ride home? We can talk there."

The offer immediately reminded her of why she couldn't drive herself home. She glanced back at her tires, wincing at the sight. "Did you see who did this?"

"No."

She eyed him doubtfully. For a second, she almost wondered if *he* had done this, but then, she couldn't think of a reason why he would. Of course, she couldn't think of a reason why he was here now, either. None of this made a bit of sense.

"You have a car?" she asked numbly.

"A truck," he said, nodding toward a black pickup parked a short distance down the street. "Come on."

He started to reach for the bags to take them from her. She shook her head, clutching them tighter, needing to hold on to something that was tangible and real.

He motioned for her to proceed in front of him. She hesitated for a moment, unsure. She needed to call someone and figure out about getting new tires. She had one spare, but she would definitely need help getting another. The thought of facing the police right now, of having to deal with this while all the unseen watchers observed and judged from their windows, was suddenly more than she could take. At the moment, she wanted nothing more than to get out of town and back to the relative safety of the ranch.

"All right," she murmured. She had no idea what he was doing here—wasn't quite convinced he wasn't some kind of illusion conjured by her desperate mind, for that matter. But right now he was offering to help her, which made him just about the only person in her world who was.

Chapter Two

"You're going to want to head right," Elena said as Matt started to back out of the parking space.

He agreed with a nod, turning as she directed without looking at her. He didn't let himself, even though it seemed like the only thing he wanted to do.

Fifteen minutes ago he hadn't seen her in years. Now she was here, sitting in his truck. She'd placed her two grocery bags on the seat between them, yet they were hardly much of a buffer. She might as well be pressed up against him, the way he felt her closeness.

He'd thought he would be prepared to see her again, thought he wouldn't feel anything after all these years. It had all been so long ago. She was nothing more than a distant memory to him, and not a particularly good one.

But good God, from the moment he'd found himself face-to-face with her, it all came back, hitting him like a blow square to the chest, the memories as vivid as though they'd happened yesterday.

Elena Reyes.

The prettiest girl he'd thought he'd ever seen. He'd thought he loved her. Whatever he'd felt back then had been the closest thing he'd ever experienced to it. He'd been a dumb kid, feeling things for the first time, *letting* himself feel those things for the first time. Back then, he'd never been able to get her out of his head. The mere sight of her had always made him happier than he'd ever been. Every time she'd smiled at him it had been like someone giving him the best present he'd ever gotten.

She hadn't been smiling the last time he'd seen her, of course. She'd been crying then. Back when she'd told him she didn't love him as much as he loved her. At least that had been the gist of it. And he'd realized he'd been a fool to feel all of those things he thought he had.

She wasn't smiling now, either. There were no tears, but her expression wasn't much brighter, her lips locked in a grim line, her eyes bleak, her features tense.

Damned if she still wasn't the prettiest thing he'd ever seen.

It didn't matter that she wasn't smiling, or that her face showed every bit of the stress she was under. It didn't even matter that it was eight years later and she was no longer the fresh-faced young woman he'd once known. If anything, the extra years had only added to her looks, delivering the full beauty that had only been hinted at when she was twenty. He'd thought she was beautiful then. If only he'd known what she would become.

Damn.

He almost wished she did look worse after all these years. It would certainly make things easier for him. He wouldn't be having this crazy reaction to a woman who really meant nothing to him. The woman who'd taught him just how foolish all those crazy emotions were in the first place.

"Okay, Matt," she said, thankfully pulling him out of his thoughts. "Now what are you doing here?"

Grateful for the reminder of the task at hand, he reached into his pocket and pulled out the envelope. "I got this in the mail," he said, holding it out to her. "Didn't you send it?"

She began to answer even before she took the envelope from him. "No, why would I?"

He could immediately tell she wasn't lying, her confusion too genuine to be faked. "I have no idea. I don't know why anybody else would, either."

"I didn't even know where you were these days," she said, flipping the envelope over and reading the address. "New Mexico?"

"That's right. Somebody around here obviously knew where I was, and I can't think of anyone besides you who would care."

"Neither can I, but it wasn't me." She waved the envelope. "What is this?"

"An article from the local paper about your husband's death."

She went still, staring at the item in her hand as though it contained something toxic and she wanted nothing more than to drop it before it contaminated her further. "Why would somebody send you that?" she whispered.

"I guess they wanted me to know about it," he said reasonably.

"But why? What purpose would that serve?"

"Only reason I could figure was that somebody wanted me to come here." He hesitated, feeling foolish for a slight second before he shoved the feeling away. "Like I said, I figured it was you."

She frowned at him. "Why would *I* send you that?"

Matt shrugged a shoulder, feeling foolish again. "I

thought maybe you needed help and were desperate enough to reach out to me of all people. From the sound of that article, things aren't looking too good for you. Maybe somebody else sent it for the same reason."

"In hopes that you'd help me?" She exhaled sharply, the sound almost like a snort. "Whatever the reason, I doubt it was good."

"What makes you say that?"

"People around here haven't exactly been going out of their way to help me out. As you may have noticed, I'm not Ms. Popularity at the moment."

He couldn't disagree with her there. He wished he'd seen who'd messed with her truck, but he'd been watching the store so closely for her to come out he hadn't been paying attention to anything else. "Has anything else happened besides someone cutting your tires?"

"That's the first outright act against me. Mostly I've been getting a cold shoulder from everyone in town. Almost no one has said a word to me since Bobby's death. Only the police." She shuddered slightly, the gesture making it clear exactly what that experience had been like for her.

He surveyed her out of the corner of his eye, this woman he hadn't seen in eight years, this person who was so familiar, yet different at the same time. She definitely wasn't the girl she'd once been. But could she have really changed enough to become a killer? It was possible. He could believe anyone was capable of killing for any number of reasons, whether out of anger or vengeance or self-defense. Was that what had happened? Had circumstances turned her into a killer? Or had she really become a far different person than the one he'd thought he'd known?

Or was it, as he'd wondered plenty of times after they parted ways, that he'd never really known her at all?

"What happened, Elena?"

She glanced at him, her left eyebrow quirking. "Didn't you read the article?"

"I'd rather hear it from you."

She simply continued to stare at him, remaining silent for a long moment. "What are you even doing here, Matt?" she repeated. "Someone sends you an article about…someone you knew a long time ago and you come all this way from New Mexico? For what?"

Someone you knew a long time ago. That was certainly an interesting way of putting it. He hadn't missed her hesitation before phrasing it that way, and he couldn't help wondering what her first instinct had been to say instead. "Guess I wanted to know why," he answered. "And yeah, I wanted to know if it was true."

"What do you care?"

"Are you saying it is?"

"No, I'm asking what difference it makes to you."

It was still a very good question. "Call it curiosity, I guess. You never struck me as a killer. Guess I wanted to know if a person could change that much."

She lowered her head, her shoulders slumping. "Thank you," she practically whispered.

"For what?"

"For thinking I'm not the killing type. People who've known me a lot longer don't even seem to believe that."

"So you're saying you didn't do it?"

"That's exactly what I'm saying," she said firmly.

"So what happened?"

Elena opened her mouth and took a deep breath, as

though on the verge of beginning, only to raise her hand and point in front of them. "In a minute. We're here."

He saw the turnoff to a ranch up ahead and smoothly guided the truck into the turn. A sign over the end of the driveway declared it the Weston Ranch. From the first glimpse, he could tell it was a big spread, wide-open pastures stretching out into the horizon. It looked like Elena had married well, he noted darkly. Not that he was surprised. He hadn't worked for them, didn't think he'd ever met any of them, but he remembered the Weston name had been big around here.

The driveway eventually ended in front of a large two-story ranch house, a barn not far from it. He could see cattle grazing in the distance in one of the pastures, a sight he knew well. She must have a lot of people working for her to be dealing with a place this size. More important, it meant there were people they were going to have to explain his presence to, something he wasn't sure just how to do.

"How many people do you have working for you right now?"

"At the moment, none."

He couldn't help but glance at her in surprise. She met his eyes and shrugged lightly, a hint of resignation in her dark brown gaze. "Nobody wants to work for a murderer."

"So how are you keeping this place running?"

"The best I can," she said simply.

As soon as he brought the truck to a stop in front of the house, she pushed her door open and climbed out, reaching back in for the bags and taking them before he could offer to help. He followed, unable to help but notice her strong, confident stride as she walked to the house and climbed the steps. She definitely wasn't a girl anymore. She was all woman, exuding a strength and grace he now saw she'd only been starting to develop back then.

Crossing the wide front porch, she opened the door. "Come on back to the kitchen," she said. "I need to get these groceries put away."

He followed her through the house, getting a quick glimpse of the living room as they passed through it. As he'd seen from the outside, it was a big place, but comfortable. Homey. The home she'd shared with her husband, he registered, the thought bothering him more than it should before he brushed the feeling aside.

In the kitchen, she put the bags on the counter and immediately began unloading them, moving some of the items to the refrigerator. There was a big table with plenty of chairs, but he remained standing, leaning against the doorway and watching her move.

Closing the refrigerator and turning away from it, she suddenly noticed him standing there and started. "I'm sorry. I'm not being a very good hostess. Can I get you something to drink?"

He gave his head a terse shake. "I'm fine. You were going to tell me what happened?"

She sighed, then nodded. "That's right. I guess I'm just not sure where to begin."

He wasn't sure he did, either. A lot of it was going to involve her relationship with her husband, a topic he didn't know if he wanted to hear all that much about, no matter how much he needed to. At the same time, he couldn't say why the idea bothered him. Or maybe he was just bothered by the implications of why it would.

"Have to admit I was surprised to find out you were

still in Western Bluff," he said. "Thought you had all those plans of being in the big city. That summer you couldn't wait to get back to school."

"I know," she said softly, without looking at him. "I never intended to stay here, either."

"So what happened?"

She shrugged helplessly. "Things changed. Bobby and I…started seeing each other, and then…things changed," she repeated weakly.

She lapsed into silence, her eyes sliding briefly to his, her discomfort with the topic etched across her face. Clearly, her relationship with her husband was just as awkward for her to talk about as it was for him to listen to.

His gut churned at her words. He'd never met Bobby Weston, not that he could remember anyway. He wished he had, wished he could know the kind of man Elena had been willing to change her life plans for when she hadn't been willing to do the same for him.

But then, he'd just been a ranch hand, offering her an uncertain life on the road. He hadn't had a spread like this to offer her. Maybe if he had, things would have been different. Maybe she would have picked him.

With a jolt of anger at himself for even thinking about it, he did his best to push the thoughts away. What did it matter? It was a long time ago. Things had happened the way they had, and there was no changing them. He had a perfectly good life, and it looked like she had, too—at least up until the point her husband was killed.

"Must have been some guy," Matt said, keeping his tone neutral.

"He was," she said quietly. "At least in the beginning. We started seeing each other…the summer after you left."

The words sent another jolt through him, and again he was irritated by his response. A year was a long time, so why did it feel like a betrayal, like she'd moved on far too quickly? It wasn't as if he'd been a monk in the year after he'd left this place—left her—behind. But then, he hadn't ended up marrying any of the women he'd been involved with, either.

Pulling out one of the chairs from the table, Elena sank into the seat. "We'd known each other, or at least known *of* each other, for years, of course. The town's too small for us not to have. I can't remember us saying two words to each other, though. He was a few years ahead of me in school, a member of one of the town's founding families, and I…wasn't. Our paths never really crossed. Then that summer I was waiting tables at the diner again, and he struck up a conversation with me. It was probably the first time he ever really noticed me. We got to talking, and we actually had some things in common.

"First and foremost, Bobby didn't want to stay in Western Bluff, either, and he wasn't supposed to. I don't know how much you heard about the Westons, or even remember if you did, but Bobby's older brother, Jim Junior, was the one who'd been groomed to take over the ranch. Bobby's father, Big Jim, died about twenty years ago when Bobby was just a boy. Junior was all of eighteen, but he managed to take over and make the ranch his own. He offered to make Bobby a place as he got older, but Bobby wasn't really interested in the ranch. The summer you were here, he had an internship at a company in Houston, so he wasn't in town. He wanted to be in the city as much as I did. The only reason he was back that summer was because Junior said he needed his help and asked Bobby to stick around. Bobby had already graduated but didn't have a job lined up yet, so he agreed."

Elena grimaced, her eyes far away. "That whole summer we talked about how we were going to get out of here. He was going to come to Austin with me when I went back to school." Matt nearly flinched at the words, at the significance of them, but managed not to. "He knew people there so he could try to find a job just as well as he could in Houston. It should have worked out perfectly. But when the summer was over, Junior asked him to stay a little longer, and made a big enough deal about it that Bobby agreed. That's when he asked me to marry him. He wanted to make things permanent, because he said there was no doubt we'd be together. And I said yes."

"How long had you been going out with him before you got married?"

Her eyes flew to his face. He met her gaze and held it. He could tell she didn't like the answer, and suspected he wasn't going to like hearing it, either.

"Three months."

He had no trouble understanding her reaction and did his best to hide his own.

Three months. The same amount of time Matt had been involved with her before they'd parted ways, before she'd refused to make the same commitment to him she'd made to another man just one year later.

"You must have really loved him," he said, instantly hearing the trace of bitterness in his own voice and hating himself for it.

She lowered her eyes. "He was crazy about me, and I—" she swallowed "—was crazy about him."

Matt didn't miss the way her voice faltered before she finished the statement, or how strained it sounded uttering those words. Were they that hard for her to admit? Or was it admitting them to him?

"I'm sure your father must have been thrilled that you got married so fast," he said wryly, remembering the man's reaction to Matt's involvement with his daughter. Ed Reyes had been so protective of his daughter Matt couldn't imagine him thinking anyone was good enough for her. Or maybe Bobby Weston's background had made him a more acceptable prospect than a humble ranch hand.

"He wasn't," she acknowledged with a sardonic smile. "We eloped and didn't tell anyone about it until it was done, and then I went back to school.

"We both thought it would only be a few months until he joined me in Austin. Instead, a few months later we found out the truth about Junior. He hadn't been feeling well, had been going to doctors to get checked out, which is why he needed Bobby's help, though he assured everyone he was fine. But he wasn't. He wasn't just sick, he was dying. He was going fast, and didn't admit it almost until the end. Then he was gone. He wasn't married and didn't have any kids, so Bobby inherited the ranch.

"At first I assumed he'd sell. But Bobby felt like he owed it to Junior to stay and run the ranch. I understood, and felt like I had to support that. His brother had just died, this was his family spread, and he was the last of the Westons. I couldn't exactly argue with him. So when I finished school, I came back, too, and we stayed."

"And you're still here," Matt summarized.

Elena nodded, more than a hint of resignation in the gesture. "Still here."

"Were you happy?"

She looked at him, her gaze steady. "No," she said flatly. "Neither of us were. After the first couple years I did begin to argue that Bobby should sell, but he wouldn't. The thing is, Big Jim was something of a local legend around here, and all his life Bobby heard about how great his father was. And then, after being the second brother, the one who wasn't expected to take over, he suddenly had pretty big shoes to fill, especially since he was the last Weston. It was a lot of pressure. At least he saw it that way, and it changed him. We had some setbacks over the years, some rough times, and Bobby took every one of them personally, as though he was failing his father and his brother. He became obsessed. The ranch was all he ever thought about. He was constantly coming up with plans and schemes to make things work better around here, none of which ever panned out, which only made things worse.

"The night he was killed, we'd had an argument. I'd pretty much had enough. Bobby had this idea to build this new irrigation system, claiming it would make things work a lot smoother around here. Of course, it would also require digging up half the spread and spending every last remaining cent we had. It was complete madness and would do nothing to solve any of the actual problems." She swallowed hard. "I told him if he intended to go through with it, I would have no choice but to leave him. I wasn't going to stand by and watch him destroy himself and what was left of our lives on his obsession with the ranch. He told me to go, because if I couldn't understand how important it was to him, then I didn't really love him anyway.

"I walked out and went for a drive to clear my head. I just needed to think about things for a while. I didn't really go anywhere, didn't think about where I was headed. I just drove until it seemed like I'd gone far enough, turned around and came back. I was gone for about four hours. When I came back, I noticed the door to his study was open and the light was still on. I almost ignored it, just wanting to go to bed and not have another confrontation, but I knew if I did he'd just stay up all night the way he did too much of the time."

Elena sucked in a breath. "That's when I found him. He was lying on his back on the floor. He'd been shot in the chest. I felt for a pulse, but he was already dead. He was still warm though. I don't know how long he'd been there. Maybe if I'd come home earlier, I could have called someone, could have saved him—"

"You can't think like that," Matt said gently. "If you'd come back earlier, the shooter could have killed you, too."

"I know," she admitted softly. "But I wish I could have done something for him. Instead, all I could do was call the police and tell them he'd been killed. Unfortunately, everyone knew that we'd been arguing, and no one else had a reason to kill him, which makes me the prime suspect. The sheriff has made it clear he thinks I'm guilty. I know he'd love to make an arrest. The only thing keeping him from doing it is a lack of physical evidence. The murder weapon was most likely a pistol that belonged to Bobby. He kept it in his gun cabinet. It's been missing since the murder. The killer must have taken it, but the sheriff is convinced I hid it somewhere, which is why he and his men have been by pretty much every other day to search the place.

"In the meantime, the hands quit. We had only a few working for us. I paid them for their work to date, but they knew I couldn't afford to keep them on. At least one made the point that I was probably going to need every penny I had for my defense."

"Sounds like somebody you're better off not having around," Matt noted.

"Most likely," Elena agreed. "But the result is that I have this ranch to run all by myself with nobody to work it, and a whole town that thinks I murdered my husband."

"Surely there have to be others who had issues with your husband, especially if the ranch was having as much trouble as you say it is."

"I've been over the books numerous times over the past week. We're low on funds and have plenty of debts, but these are held by banks and certainly wouldn't be worth killing him over. And while not everybody in town necessarily loved him, I haven't been able to come up with anyone with serious enough issues to want to do him harm. Believe me, I've been racking my brain trying to think of a single possibility."

"What about these hands you had working for you? Weren't any of them around that night? Didn't any of them see anything?"

"No. They'd all gone to town. Bobby had given them the day off."

"Convenient," Matt said. "That strike anybody as odd?"

Elena shrugged. "Not really. Afterward I kind of wondered if he suspected this blowout between us was coming and didn't want anyone around to overhear. It had been building for some time," she admitted.

"Is it possible one of the hands killed him? Maybe they were worried about getting paid?"

"They were all in town at the bar. They have alibis."

Her voice was thick with frustration. He could understand why. The situation certainly didn't look good. But listening to her, he didn't have a doubt in the world that she was telling the truth. She was no murderer. Whatever else might have changed about her over the years, that hadn't. Which meant she needed help. She might not have sent the article to him—he definitely believed her about that, too—but the result was the same.

Before he could say anything, the sound of an engine reached them, drawing their attention toward the front of the house. Someone was coming up the driveway.

Matt glanced back at her. "Expecting company?"

Her heavy frown answered before she did. "No," she said, rising from her chair.

He pushed away from the door frame, ready to follow. "Any idea who it could be?"

"Not really," she said, moving past him. "But if there's one thing I've learned by now, it's bound to be trouble."

Chapter Three

She'd been right, Elena reflected grimly as she watched the two men climb out of the police vehicle they'd parked in front of the house. It was trouble.

Sheriff Walt Bremer climbed out first, heaving himself from behind the driver's seat with a great deal of effort. In his mid-fifties, he was a big man in every way, increasingly around his midsection. He'd always been pleasant enough to Elena and she'd never had any issues with him before. But once he'd zeroed in on her as his prime suspect, he'd turned on her so thoroughly it was hard to believe he'd ever had a kind word for her in the past.

A second, equally familiar man emerged from the passenger seat. Travis Gerard—Cassie's husband, Bobby's best friend since they were boys, and a local deputy. He was thirty, like Bobby had been, a long, lean figure with close-cropped hair and dark eyes. Like Cassie, he was someone she'd socialized with numerous times over the years due to his friendship with Bobby. But their relationship had started out cool and only grown cooler at the same time her marriage had, understandably enough. As Bobby's best friend, she knew he'd been treated to plenty of Bobby's complaining about her over the years, how she wasn't supporting him, how she was too concerned about money. Once he'd actually pulled her aside and tried to play marriage counselor, by telling her she had a responsibility to be there for Bobby. She hadn't been in the mood to explain Bobby's latest bright idea, and hadn't really thought it was any of his business, so her lack of cooperation had likely only lowered his opinion of her. He'd been cold enough toward her when it seemed like she wasn't getting along with Bobby. Unsurprisingly, now that it seemed that she'd killed him, Travis was hellbent on making her pay.

As they approached, she saw that the men's interest wasn't in her, but in the man standing at her side, and she knew immediately why they'd come. Her interaction with Matt in town, and the fact that she'd driven off with him, hadn't gone unnoticed. The sheriff no doubt wanted to know who Matt was—and what he was doing with Elena.

For a second, she felt a flicker of apprehension. She hadn't thought about the outside impact of Matt's presence here. If their prior relationship came out, the fact that he'd come back to town so soon after Bobby's death could look very bad—for both of them.

Before she could begin to sort through the ramifications and how to deal with the issue, the men had reached the house. "Afternoon, Elena," Walt said with a pleasantness that couldn't have been more fake.

She made the immediate decision to go on the offensive. Once again, she couldn't afford to look the slightest bit weak or guilty. "Good afternoon, Sheriff. Travis," she said, nodding to the younger man in turn. She noticed he didn't bother looking at her, his attention fixed on Matt, eyes narrowed with clear suspicion. "I'm glad to see you both."

The briefest flash of surprise crossed across Walt's face. "Oh, you are, are you?"

"Of course. You're here about my truck, right?"

"What about it?"

"Oh, I thought you might be here because someone slashed my tires when I was in town a little while ago."

The sheriff's eyebrows shot sky high. "That's a pretty serious allegation, Elena. You have any proof?"

"Two tires don't just go flat for no reason."

Walt shrugged one shoulder. "Stranger things have happened."

"But I'm sure you'll investigate to find out what really happened, won't you, Sheriff?"

"I'm a little busy trying to solve Bobby's murder at the moment to waste time on a minor nuisance matter. I'm sure that's where you'd prefer my resources to be focused—catching your husband's killer, isn't it, Elena?"

His cloying tone made it sound like he'd caught her in some kind of trap. She simply stared back at him, unyielding. "Of course. I'd like nothing more than for you to catch the actual person responsible for killing Bobby."

Walt's expression turned sardonic, clearly saying he saw what she was implying and he wasn't fooled by her in the least. But when he spoke what he said was, "Aren't you going to introduce us to your friend, Elena?"

She almost started. For a moment, she'd actually managed to forget Matt was even there.

Before she could figure out how to explain Matt's presence and who he was, Matt answered first.

"Mrs. Weston just hired me to help her out around here."

It was all Elena could do not to snap her head toward him in surprise. Instead, she did her best not to let her reaction show, not wanting to tip off the policemen that it was a lie when that would only look more suspicious.

It turned out she didn't need to worry. Walt and Travis never took their eyes off Matt, Walt's expression becoming contemplative, Travis's plainly hostile.

"Help her out with what?" Travis asked, a sneer in his tone.

"The ranch," Matt said smoothly without missing a beat. "It sounded like she could use some help around here with things."

"Did she tell you why she needed help?" Walt asked, the question clearly leading somewhere.

"Her husband recently died and the men he'd had working for him moved on."

"Did she tell you her husband was murdered?" Travis demanded. "Shot to death in that very house? Or did you already know that?"

"As a matter of fact, she did tell me that," Matt said.

"And that doesn't make you nervous about working for her? It sure scared off the rest of the hands."

"I guess I'm made of stronger stuff than they are."

"What's your name again?" the sheriff asked, even though they all knew full well Matt hadn't offered it.

"Alvarez," Matt said. "Matt Alvarez."

Deciding she'd had enough of this, Elena spoke up. "Is there something I can help you with, Sheriff? Something must have brought you out here, since you didn't come about my truck."

Walt smiled thinly. "We just thought we'd stop by

and see if you remembered anything else about the night Bobby was murdered."

"No, I haven't," she said simply.

"In that case, I guess we'll be going."

He shot one final glance at Matt, then turned and headed back to his car. It took a moment for Travis to do the same, glaring at Matt, then Elena before following the sheriff.

She and Matt didn't speak as the two men climbed back in their vehicle. They watched in silence as the sheriff backed up, then headed down the driveway.

When the car was nearly out of sight, Elena finally spoke. "Why did you tell them that?"

"As soon as I saw who it was, I figured we were going to have to explain what I was doing here. That seemed like the best explanation."

"But now it'll look bad if you don't stay."

"I'm not going anywhere, not until I have some answers."

The determination in his voice sent a shudder down her spine. "I'm not sure your staying here is a good idea."

"Why not?"

"If anyone finds out about our…prior relationship," she said delicately, "it will look really bad that you suddenly showed up so soon after Bobby's murder and are staying here."

"It's been eight years. I doubt anybody will remember. I was nothing more than a ranch hand passing through, and we were careful about not being too public because you didn't want your father finding out, remember? Only a few people knew in the end anyway. Are the Nolans still around?" he asked, referring to the people who'd owned the ranch where he'd worked that summer.

"No, they sold out a few years ago," she admitted.

"What about Weston? Would he have told anybody about me?"

She glanced away. "I don't think he knew. I never told him and he never mentioned it."

"So it's unlikely anyone remembered."

"Small towns have long memories, especially this one. And at least one person in town clearly knows."

"Somebody who probably wanted to help you. Why else would they send me that article?"

"To cause trouble for me? Like I said, it could look bad having you here. Not to mention, how could they know you would come here to help me if they sent you a newspaper article?"

"Guess the only way to find out what that person's motives are is to find out who it is. Another reason for me to stick around."

She eyed him doubtfully, unable to shake the notion that this was a bad idea. The idea of having him here, so close at hand. Yes, she could use the help, if that was what he was truly here for. If the incident with her tires was any indication, it might be a good thing to have someone nearby.

But having this particular man, with his inexplicable motives and dark, compelling eyes, so close suddenly seemed infinitely more dangerous.

He met her gaze seriously. "Look, if you don't want me staying here, that's your call. This is your place. I can't force myself on you or your property. I can try to find somewhere in town to stay. But I'm not going anywhere until I have some answers. I want to know who sent me that article—and yes, why."

Elena felt her resistance—and most likely, her common sense—weakening. Yes, it could be a bad idea to have him here. No, she didn't understand what he was doing here, or why he would want to help her. But she believed he wanted answers, and with the rest of the town seemingly having already made up their minds, that gave them a common goal. Perhaps that was reason enough to keep him close, despite all the reasons she wasn't sure she should.

"All right," she said softly. "You can stay."

If he wondered why she'd caved, he didn't show it, simply nodding once. "Good. I was thinking we should go back into town and get your truck."

Elena automatically frowned at the suggestion. She was in no hurry to go back into Western Bluff after her last visit, especially so soon. But as she considered the idea, she realized he was right. They shouldn't leave her truck sitting on Main Street. God only knew what someone might do to it in the middle of the night, or if it would even be there the next day. Even if it were, she wouldn't put it past Walt or Travis to give her a parking ticket or trump up some other infraction just to cause her trouble.

"We'll need to change the tires," she noted.

"Do you have any spares?"

"There's one in the truck bed, and a few others in the barn."

He nodded. "Great. I'll load a couple in my truck and we can go."

"I'll show you where they are in the barn."

He automatically turned and headed in that direction. Elena waited a few seconds before following, watching him walk away with that same strange sense of unreality washing over her again. Her whole world seemed to have been upended again in a mere hour. It didn't seem possible that this was happening, yet evidently it was.

Matt Alvarez was back in her life, as suddenly as he'd once left it.

And it seemed, for the moment at least, this time he intended to stay.

Chapter Four

"Tell me about the sheriff," Matt said as they headed back into town.

Elena glanced over at him from the passenger's seat, grateful he'd raised the subject—any subject. Anything to distract her from her still unsteady emotions, and his closeness in the truck's cab. "All right. What do you want to know?"

He kept his eyes on the road, his profile hard as stone. "Is he good at his job?"

Elena considered the question. "I've always figured he was. Walt's been the sheriff for, I'd say, at least six years now, and he was a deputy for years before that."

"So there's a chance he might remember me from back then."

Elena frowned at the memory. "There's a chance," she agreed.

"We can worry about that when we need to. Ever had any trouble with him before?"

"None. I didn't have that much direct interaction with him, and when I did, he was always nice enough to me. When I was a teenager, there were a few times when he brought my father home, and he was always nice about it." Too nice, she thought with a trace of irritation. The kind of niceness that was really just pity. Far too many people had looked at her like that back then, if they'd acknowledged her existence at all.

Poor girl. Mother took off. Father's a drunk.

Of course, that was a lot better than the way people were looking at her now, she thought, as a grim smile touched her lips. She'd never imagined a day when being Ed Reyes's outcast daughter would seem like a step up to her. Or maybe that was the natural progression of things in some way. She'd turned out to be the bad seed her disreputable beginning had always made them think she'd be.

"So there's no reason to believe this is personal for him and he's not just trying to do his job."

"Not for him, no."

"But for someone else?" he concluded. "The deputy?"

"Travis is—*was*," she corrected with a wince, "Bobby's best friend. Was ever since they were little kids."

"No wonder he's gunning for you, if he thinks you killed him."

"It probably doesn't help that he never liked me to begin with."

"Why not?"

"He didn't think I was good enough for Bobby. But then, most people didn't. After all, he was a Weston. His great-great-grandfather was one of the founders of this town and Bobby's family was practically royalty around here. People used to say the town should have been called 'Weston's Bluff.' He was golden in this town. He could have had any girl he wanted."

"And he wanted you."

She didn't say anything for a moment. "Yes," she

said, her tone distant. "He did. In the beginning, at least."

As soon as she'd said the last words, she wished she could take them back. There was too much she didn't want to get into, things she didn't want to explain.

But if he wondered what had changed, he didn't ask. Maybe he didn't want to know any more than she wanted to get into it. A tiny bit of relief pierced her uneasiness.

"Did you ever think there might be another reason one of them is so determined to pin the murder on you?" he asked.

"What do you mean?"

"What if one of them is the killer?"

The idea was so absurd she nearly laughed. "Neither of them have motives."

"That you know of. You said nobody had a motive to kill your husband, but clearly somebody must have. After all, if you didn't kill him, somebody did, and there had to have been a reason. You just don't know what it is."

He was right, of course. She'd spent more than one sleepless night wondering who had killed Bobby—and why. The first answer depended on the second, but she hadn't had any luck answering either one, hadn't even come up with any remote possibilities. Rather than find a solution to her situation, her efforts had merely confirmed how dire it was.

She tried to wrap her mind around the idea of Walt or Travis killing Bobby in cold blood. It just didn't make sense, and not just for the lack of motive.

"If it were Walt or Travis, then why wouldn't they have left the gun, or planted it somewhere they could claim to have found it? Somewhere that would have made me look bad? The fact that the gun is missing is one of the only things keeping them from making an arrest. If one of them is the killer, then that person has the gun."

He fell silent for a moment, and she sensed him considering her words. "I don't know," he finally said. "That's a good point. I'm just trying to keep an open mind. We can't dismiss any possibility out of hand, no matter how far-fetched. We can't afford to overlook anything or anyone, not if we want to get to the bottom of this."

He was right, she acknowledged. This was the way it had to be. Sure, it didn't seem like anyone had a motive to kill Bobby, but someone clearly had. Until they figured out who it was, everyone had to be looked at as though they could be the killer.

It was only fair. After all, that was how everybody in town was looking at her.

"Okay," Matt said, pushing himself to his feet. "You're good to go."

Elena glanced at the two fully inflated tires, the truck now perfectly balanced on all four. "Thank you. Let's get out of here."

Matt had no trouble understanding her relief. He'd had his attention on the tires most of the time since they'd arrived back at her truck, but he'd been able to feel people watching them. No one had approached or said a word. It hadn't mattered. He'd known they were there. It wasn't a comfortable feeling.

Still, he wasn't ready to retreat just yet. Getting her truck fixed had been just the first item on his agenda when they got to town. He had other business to take care of.

"You go on ahead," he told her. "I want to poke around here a bit."

Her attention already drifting to the street and their unseen watchers, she turned back to him in surprise. Not that there was any reason for her to be surprised. It was, after all, what he was here for.

As if realizing it, she slowly nodded. "All right."

"I'll see you back at the house."

He waited, expecting her to turn and get into the truck. She didn't. She simply stood there, her eyes searching his face, her expression suddenly uncertain. It seemed as though she wanted to say something else.

And in an instant, he understood.

They were already saying goodbye, so soon after meeting again after so long. The strangeness of it hit him. It had always felt strange saying goodbye to her. He'd never been quite ready to do it. It didn't matter that they would see each other again in a little while. Or was she wondering if that was true, if she should say something, a more definitive goodbye than the last time, just in case?

This was actually a lot like the last time they'd said goodbye. They'd been on the street, not too far from here in fact. The difference was it had been night.

And they'd both had no reason to think he was ever coming back.

He *was* coming back, he almost felt like reassuring her. But he knew it wouldn't matter. Some part of her still wasn't ready to say goodbye to him, any more than it ever had been. And he realized maybe he wasn't ready, either, as the same innate sense of connection he'd had with this woman from the first moment he'd seen her clicked deep within him.

Eight years. It should have been long enough to wash away whatever feelings he'd once had for this woman. But as he peered down into the eyes staring back at him, took in her upturned face, he felt it just the same.

Whatever she might have wanted to say, she didn't. With another tight nod, she finally turned and rounded the front of the truck to the driver's side.

Stepping away from the vehicle, Matt watched her climb in and start the engine. He remained where he was as she backed out of the space. There was no reason for him to stay there. He needed to get going, needed to get started poking around.

But something held him in place, and he watched her drive away, the truck slowly heading down the street and fading into the distance.

"She's not somebody you really want to get mixed up with."

Matt recognized the voice without seeing the speaker behind him. It was the deputy who'd come by Elena's ranch earlier—Travis, she'd said his name was. He had the same sneer in his voice.

The man's tone rankled. The fact that Matt wasn't sure he disagreed with the statement did, too.

Not letting his expression show the slightest reaction, Matt slowly turned to face the man.

The sneer was on the deputy's face, as well. He peered at Matt, eyes narrowed as they studied him, like the guy was trying to figure him out. The scrutiny lasted long enough Matt was sure the man hadn't managed it.

"Is that so?" Matt said mildly.

"She's a murderer. Killed her husband in cold blood. Is that really somebody you want to be working for?"

"I figure if you had any proof against her she'd be locked up already."

"It's only a matter of time," Travis practically spat. "Everybody in this town knows she did it, and nobody's going to let her get away with it."

"Well, until that happens, she's still somebody with a job that needs to be done."

"As soon as she's locked up, you might find it hard getting paid for whatever work you've done."

"Guess I'll worry about that when the time comes."

The man grimaced, his mouth tightening with barely controlled anger. "Even if you don't believe she's a killer, take my word, she's no good. Probably no surprise there—her family wasn't, either."

The man let the comment hang in the air, probably expecting Matt to be curious enough to ask for more details. Heck, most people probably would be after a comment like that. But Matt already knew all about Elena's family. He'd met Ed Reyes himself, knew full well what kind of man he was. And Elena herself had told him more than this man could begin to, just as he'd told her things...

Not that he could admit that to this man. But even if he could, he wasn't about to. He didn't like bullies, never had. And Travis Gerard had *bully* written all over him. It made Matt wonder what kind of man Elena's husband had been, if this was the type of person he'd considered his best friend in the world. Matt's reflexive dislike for Bobby Weston grew deeper.

"Her old man was a drunk," the deputy finally said when the silence went on too long. "Her mother took off when she was just a kid. With a background like that, probably makes sense that she wouldn't consider her own marriage worth much."

"What's your point?"

"I'd think you'd want to know the kind of person you're working for."

"Why would her family make a difference when it comes to working for her? That's her family, not her."

Travis Gerard's eyes narrowed, fresh contempt shining from them. "So you're that kind of guy, huh? Doesn't matter what kind of person you work for?"

"I'm just wondering why you're wasting your time trying to scare me off. What does it matter to you if I get paid or not?"

"Her husband was a good friend of mine. I don't like the idea of her out there, going about her life like nothing happened, like she didn't kill a good man in cold blood."

"Then prove she did it," Matt said. "Trying to scare me off isn't going to get that done."

The deputy's face went dark red, his whole body tensing, and for a second, Matt was positive the man wanted nothing more than to deck him, was just about ready to throw that punch.

Matt held his ground, not about to back down, ready to take the blow if he had to. He was ready and willing to go toe to toe with this arrogant ass, but raising a hand against a Texas deputy was a surefire way to get in trouble, and there wasn't much he could do for Elena if he landed in jail his first day in town.

Finally, Gerard took a step back, giving his chin a belligerent tilt. "Don't say I didn't warn you."

"Don't worry, Deputy," Matt returned coolly. "I consider myself warned."

With a curl of his lip, Gerard turned on his heel and stomped away.

Matt watched him go, the knot of tension in the pit of his stomach only tightening. He didn't feel the slightest bit of relief that the deputy had backed down, his awareness of just how bad the situation was weighing down on him too heavily.

Whether or not Travis Gerard was right about the rest of the town—and the slashed tires indicated he just might be—the fact that the local law was gunning for Elena was confirmation enough that she needed help. Damned if he was going to stand by and watch her be railroaded. Unfortunately, she probably needed more help than he alone could offer, he had to admit. Luckily he might know someone who could provide some assistance.

Climbing into his truck, he pulled the envelope out of his pocket, found a pen in the glove compartment, then reached for his phone, hitting the speed dial.

A familiar voice answered after a few rings. "Triple C."

"Piper, it's Matt."

"Matt, where are you? Is everything okay?"

"Everything's fine," he said, dodging the first question. "I just need you to give me Pam's phone number."

She didn't say anything for a long moment, and he braced himself for her answer. "Everything can't be fine if you want to talk to an FBI agent."

"I just have a little bit of a situation here and I'm hoping she'd be willing to do something for me."

"Is there anything Cade and I can do to help?"

He had no doubt that if he said the word, she and Cade would hightail it to Western Bluff as fast as they could, no questions asked. That was the kind of people they were, not just the people he worked for but his closest friends in the world. "You can give me Pam's phone number," he said simply.

She fell quiet again, then slowly began to recite the digits. He immediately jotted them down on the back of the envelope. "Do you need me to repeat it?" she asked when she was done.

"No, I got it."

"We're here if you need us, Matt."

"I know," he said gently. "I appreciate that, Piper."

"Take care of yourself," she said, then disconnected the phone.

Swallowing a sigh, he dialed the number she'd just given him and waited for someone to answer.

The call was picked up on the third ring. "This is Pam," a voice almost exactly like the one he'd just spoken to said in a no-nonsense tone.

"Pam, it's Matt Alvarez."

She fell silent for a few moments much like her sister had. "Matt," she said flatly, her voice devoid of Piper's natural warmth. "This is a surprise." She gave no indication whether it was pleasant or otherwise.

"I'm sorry to bother you, but I'm in a situation and could use your help."

"What is it?" He quickly outlined Elena's circumstances. "This case doesn't fall within federal jurisdiction," she said when he was finished. "There's nothing I can do officially."

"I know that. I was just hoping for some information."

"What kind of information?"

"For now, anything you can give me on the town, on Elena and her husband, the sheriff and whether he can be trusted. Obviously, you have resources that I don't. I'm not asking for anything illegal or that would get you into trouble. Just anything you can give me that you think I need to know, though I might need to come back to you later the more I learn here."

She didn't say anything for a long moment again. "This woman must mean a lot to you."

His mind instantly wanted to deny the idea. Elena didn't mean anything to him. Not anymore.

He couldn't exactly say that. It would raise far more questions, ones he wasn't sure he was ready for and didn't like the answers to.

Instead, he simply said, "She's a friend."

Another silence. When she spoke again, all she said was "Give me a number where I can reach you." Matt quickly gave it to her. "I'll see what I can find."

"Thank you," he said, only to realize she'd already hung up. With most people the action would probably be considered rude, but he didn't take any offense at it. That was Pam—brisk, blunt, to the point. She was willing to help. That was all he cared about.

Lowering his phone, he glanced up, his eyes suddenly meeting those of a woman standing down the street a short distance away.

He could tell she'd been watching him for a while, her face reflecting surprise at having been caught. If he hadn't been so focused on the call with Pam he might have sensed it. Still, she didn't immediately glance away, continuing to look at him. He looked right back. Given the way he'd felt people watching him since he and Elena had arrived back here to change her tires, he figured he should get used to people staring at him. That didn't mean he was going to let them think they could intimidate him or make him in any way nervous.

But as he absorbed the woman's attention, he realized it was different somehow. She was an attractive woman in her fifties with dark hair and eyes and a nice face. There was a warmth to it, and her attention wasn't cold or judgmental. It was like she was studying him closely, looking for something. He half wondered what it was, not caring all that much. Maybe she was just curious about a stranger. It didn't seem like she meant him any harm, and as long as that remained the case, she could look as long as she wanted.

As though finally realizing just how long she had been staring, she abruptly looked away and started down the sidewalk in the other direction.

He watched her go for a few seconds before shaking his head and dismissing her strange behavior. He had bigger things to worry about.

Pam could likely get information that he couldn't, but he'd meant what he'd said. He intended to learn as much here as he could. It might still be early enough that word hadn't gotten out about who he was and why he was supposedly in town, so there might still be time to find someone willing to talk to him. And there was one place around here he figured was his best bet to find someone who would.

Chapter Five

Her hands were shaking.

The realization came with a strange sense of detachment, as though she was noticing something that was happening to someone else. Elena glanced down at the hands that were gripping the steering wheel tightly. Yes, they were shaking, she registered, barely feeling it. The steering wheel was shuddering beneath them.

No, she corrected faintly. Her hands weren't shaking. Her whole body was.

She looked back up at the road, only to discover that she was already outside of town. Blinking in shock, she tried to draw in a breath. It was impossible. Her lungs were too tight.

She quickly swung over to the side of the road and sat there, still clutching the steering wheel in a death grip, trying to catch that elusive breath. Thankfully, there were no other vehicles in view, no one in front of or behind her, no one to witness her meltdown. She was alone, truly alone for the first time since Matt's sudden reappearance in her life.

She wasn't surprised that she'd managed to get all the way outside of town without noticing where she was. From the moment she'd driven away from him, there'd been only one thing on her mind.

Matt.

Matt was back.

The image of the way he'd looked on the street came back to her.

She hadn't wanted to say goodbye. Not again. Not yet.

Suddenly, the flood of memories she'd barely managed to keep at bay when he was near finally broke free, filling her head with a million different thoughts, pictures, impressions. Things she hadn't thought about in years. Things she hadn't let herself.

Eight years. She could feel every one of the years that had passed since he'd left, and yet it seemed as vivid as if it were yesterday.

She'd been working at the diner that summer. She hadn't wanted to come back to Western Bluff, but she'd needed to save as much money as possible for school and it hadn't made sense to pay rent for an apartment when that money could be saved. Even with the scholarship she'd managed to get, she was barely making her way through college as it was. So she'd come home and waited tables. She'd worked at the diner all through high school, having been forced early on to get a job. Not only had she known she was going to have to pay her own way through college if she wanted to get out of this town, but her father hadn't been the most reliable of providers. She'd spent too many years experiencing the fear of not knowing if the bills would be paid and their needs would be met. College was her number-one priority, but if push came to shove, she would have something to dip into to cover any shortfall.

Lavonne had been nice enough to keep a job open for her and hire her on over the summers. The diner's owner had been the closest thing Elena had had to a mother figure after her own mother abandoned them. If there was one person Elena could imagine sending Matt the newspaper article to bring him back to help her, it was Lavonne, but she'd died five years ago, shortly after Ed.

It had been a fairly typical night. She'd been doing her best to stave off the boredom and her unhappiness about being in this town she'd hated so much, just trying to make it to the end of her shift, dreaming about being back at school.

He'd come in with a few other hands from the Nolan ranch. It wasn't uncommon for hands from the area ranches to make their way into town on their nights off. Lord knew there wasn't much else around here. Usually, they'd hit the bar on the edge of town, then make their way to the diner for dessert if they needed to sober up a bit before making their way home. Most of them would flirt with her. She'd always be friendly, keeping her tips in mind, but not *too* friendly. She had no interest in cowboys, in any guys from the area for that matter. Her future lay far from here, and she was too aware of that fact to get overly attached to anything she found here.

She hadn't seen him or his group when he'd come in, only registered that some people had. After finishing with the table she'd been taking care of, she'd picked up a few menus from the counter and turned to head over to the newcomers.

And then she'd seen him.

He'd been sitting at the corner booth with three other

cowboys, but he was the only one she saw. He was beautiful. Not in a way that she ever would have associated with that word before. He wasn't pretty. There certainly wasn't anything feminine about him. He was young, in his early twenties, not much older than she was, but there was no denying he was a man. He had thick black hair and deep bronze skin, his features strong and masculine. It wasn't a flawless face, not in the conventional sense. He was no model. No, he was too real, his face had too much character. And yes, to her eyes, he was, quite simply, beautiful.

Whether he'd sensed her attention or simply chosen to raise his head at that moment, he'd suddenly looked up, his eyes automatically and unerringly meeting hers.

In an instant, everything around them seemed to disappear, leaving only the two of them, looking at each other. Even across the restaurant she'd seen his eyes widen slightly. To an outsider, it might have looked like the reaction was surprise, and maybe that was part of it. But only a small part. Because staring into his eyes, she felt it, the same thing he must have, a click deep inside, an instantaneous connection, a cord formed between them and pulled taut.

Yes.

She didn't hear the word in her head so much as she felt it deep in her body, every cell sighing with rightness as she looked into this man's eyes.

Yes.

She knew immediately that he wasn't the kind of guy she was looking for. She didn't want a cowboy. She didn't want anyone even remotely connected to this town.

She also knew immediately that it didn't matter. Be-

cause the moment she saw him, the moment their eyes
met, she knew. Whatever this was, it was right.

Yes.

She'd done her best to do her job and not let the rest
of his table see her response to him, even as she felt
his eyes on her every time she was in the main room of
the diner, even as she couldn't stop sneaking glances at
him every possible moment. And every time, he'd be
looking back at her.

He'd lingered after they'd paid the check and the
rest of his friends stepped outside, waiting at the end
of the counter for her. She'd known why, too, as she
walked over to him.

He'd leaned close. "Can I see you later?" he asked,
low under his breath, directly into her ear, and she'd
nearly shuddered. "Maybe give you a ride home?"

"Sure." She hardly lived far enough away to need a
ride, but she wasn't about to turn down the offer.

"What time do you get off work?"

"Midnight." She'd told him about a spot at the end of
the block, instinctively knowing she didn't want word
getting out—getting back to her father—that she'd met
some cowboy after work and driven off with him. That
spot was close enough to be convenient, yet far enough
away no one should pay much attention.

"I'll be there," he'd promised.

She should have been nervous. He was a complete
stranger, and undeniably a man. She knew nothing
about him. The prospect of being alone with him should
have made her wary. But it hadn't.

She'd almost been afraid he wouldn't be there, that
he'd change his mind. She'd hurried there after work,
trying not to run, not wanting to look too eager.

He'd been waiting for her, in the shadows at the end of the block, a corner the nearest streetlamp didn't quite reach. He'd stepped out into the light when he'd seen her, his strong, sensual lips curving into a smile that took her breath away. And by the time she reached him she'd been smiling, too.

"I'm glad you came," he said, his voice low and deep, incredibly sexy.

"Me, too," she said. His truck was parked behind him. She waited for him to offer to help her in, maybe even make some pointless small talk about how the rest of her shift had gone.

Instead, there in the shadowed darkness at the end of the block, he'd kissed her.

It wasn't what she'd expected. She hadn't been ready for it. But as soon as his lips met hers she knew it was exactly right.

He'd kissed her, long and slow and sweetly, like she'd never been kissed before. She might as well not have been. Nothing she'd experienced before could begin to compare.

Things didn't get any less heady as the summer went on. They'd had to sneak around. She hadn't wanted her father to find out about them. He had never liked the idea of her dating. To call him overprotective would have been the understatement of the century. It wasn't just the usual protectiveness of a father toward his daughter, his only child. He'd watched her like a hawk ever since her mother had left them without a word. Elena had known he'd been afraid of losing her, too, had considered anyone who might take her away from him a threat. His drinking hadn't exactly made him any more rational about the matter, either. It had been a miracle he'd let her go away to school, but even that had required a great deal of arguing, until he'd realized she was going, and the only way to hold on to her at all would be to let her. And even then he'd made it seem like a betrayal.

So they'd seen each other in secret, whenever Matt could get away from the ranch, which wasn't nearly enough for either of them. Nights when she worked at the diner he would wait for her at their corner. At first he would drive her home, then they began to stay out later together. Her father was usually too out of it to notice. They would talk, and kiss, and when the time came that she was ready and couldn't wait anymore, they finally made love on a blanket stretched out on a field under the stars.

She'd never dated much in high school—never had the time—and had seen only a few guys casually in college. This was so much more than any of those fleeting experiences. They'd shared everything about their lives, her more than him at first. She'd told him about life with her father, about her mother leaving, the most ridiculously insignificant little details about her life. And he'd listened to every word, patiently.

"I just like hearing your voice," he'd told her once, the words warming her as none ever had.

He'd told her he'd never been close to his parents, either, and didn't have a relationship with them, though he wouldn't tell her why, simply saying it was complicated. It was only after a couple months, almost at the end of their time together, that he'd finally told her the details late one night. How he'd been raised by his mother, who'd moved them around various small towns in the Southwest. His father had been a rodeo cowboy she'd fallen hard for. He hadn't stuck around, not wanting a kid, and his mother had blamed Matt for ruining her life. It hadn't helped that he'd looked like his father, and every time she saw him she saw the face of someone she hated. He'd been the target of all her rages, until he'd done everything he could to get away from home. In one of the towns where they'd lived, there'd been a ranch nearby, and he'd spent hours by himself standing outside the fence watching the horses. When he was twelve he'd gotten a job mucking out stalls at another ranch, and gradually he'd learned more about horses and the cattle business, though he never got to stay anywhere for long. Eventually, his mother would be ready to move on.

He'd come home one night when he was fifteen to find his mother packing to leave with her latest boyfriend. She wasn't coming back, he wasn't invited. He hadn't been sorry to see her go. He'd been on his own ever since, managing to get hired on at ranches by lying about his age.

He'd met his father once, managing to track him down. It was like his mother had said, Matt looked a lot like him. There was no denying they were father and son. Except that was exactly what the man had done. He'd cussed Matt out, told him to take a hike, threatened to kick his ass if he didn't get the hell away from him. Not figuring the man was worth the trouble, he'd done just that.

His voice had been flat and controlled as he'd told it, but she'd been able to detect the emotion in his voice, the deep pain beneath the stoic exterior. She'd known, even before he admitted it, that he'd never told anyone else about any of that before. Only her. Because he trusted her. Because he loved her.

He'd told her that, too—finally—after several months. She knew the admission hadn't come easy, the vulnerability it required everything he'd learned to protect himself against. When she'd said it back, she'd seen the joy in his face, but also the relief, and it had broken her heart a little. She wondered if anyone had ever said that to him before. Everything inside her told her they hadn't.

They'd both been alone and basically on their own for most of their lives. But they weren't alone anymore. Now they had each other.

After a few brief, uneasy exchanges about the subject, they'd avoided talking about the future, about what would happen at the end of the summer when she went back to school. It didn't matter. She knew they'd work it out somehow. They'd found each other. They loved each other. There was no way they ever wouldn't be together.

Remembering it now, Elena shook her head. God, she'd been young. And so foolish.

Then her father had found out about them. She'd never discovered how, but she supposed by the end they'd been less careful than they'd once been. Nothing had mattered but being with him; every minute they'd been apart from each other had been unbearable.

Her father had erupted. He'd actually gone to the police to complain about the man messing around with his daughter, though she'd been an adult and obviously there was nothing they could have charged Matt with, even if they'd been inclined to bother.

But then her father had gone out to the Nolan ranch where Matt was working that summer. From what she'd heard in the whispers people hadn't managed to hide entirely behind her back, he'd made a fool of himself, screaming and flailing and demanding that Matt be fired, threatening to come back as much as he needed to until it happened. Unfortunately, he'd gotten what he'd wanted. Tom Nolan had a spread to run, and neither the time nor the interest to put up with Ed Reyes's nonsense. Even if he called the police to have him hauled away, Ed would have been back as promised once he drank enough. The summer was almost over, the season was winding down, and Matt was just another hand. It really wasn't worth the hassle of dealing with Ed to keep him around.

So he'd been let go. And there'd been nothing for him to do but leave town.

He'd asked her to come with him.

She'd said no.

A decision that had seemed like the right one—the only one possible at the time.

A decision she'd reconsidered more often than she could count.

The sunlight suddenly hit her eyes, blinding her. Raising a hand to shade them, she glanced up, gradually realizing where she was. She was still in her truck, parked on the side of the road. She must have been sitting there for a while. The sun had moved, sinking lower in the sky until it finally hit her face. A glance at the clock confirmed it. More than a half hour had passed.

With a sigh, she tried to shake off the remnants of the memories. She couldn't sit here all day. The longer she remained on the side of the road, the more likely someone would notice. She was lucky no one had passed by already. The last thing she needed was for word to get out that she'd been parked on the highway, having some kind of breakdown. Not to mention there was more than enough work waiting for her back at the ranch. She was only just managing to do the bare minimum to keep things going around there on her own.

Starting the engine, she shifted the truck into gear and pulled out onto the road. So much to do, beginning with learning how to put the past behind her and get her emotions under control. As long as Matt was here, it was something she was going to have to do. She had enough to worry about. She didn't have the time or energy to waste wallowing in the past.

He was just a friend. Here to help her.

She couldn't afford to think of him as anything else.

EIGHT YEARS AGO THERE'D ONLY been one bar in town. Matt had no trouble finding it on the edge of town just off the main street. There were no vehicles in the parking lot when he pulled in. It wasn't even five o'clock, he realized. Maybe too early to expect anyone to be here.

Sure enough, the place was almost empty except for one man seated—more like slumped over—at the bar, and one standing behind it. The seated man didn't react to Matt's entrance, though the bartender looked up. He appeared to be in his forties. Matt didn't recognize him, which might not mean much. If he was hoping people wouldn't remember him, there was a good chance he wouldn't remember everyone he'd met in Western Bluff eight years ago. Still, something told him he didn't know this man.

With a nod, Matt walked up to the bar and slid onto a stool. "Afternoon."

"Afternoon," the bartender said simply. "What can I get you?"

"A beer'd be good. Whatever you have on tap."

With a nod, the bartender moved away. The man certainly wasn't overly friendly, something that wasn't going to help Matt with his mission. He was going to have to hope tipping well would open the man up. Reaching for his wallet, he pulled out a twenty.

"You new around here?"

It wasn't the bartender who'd spoken, but the man seated a couple stools down from Matt. Matt glanced over at him, taking in the way he was hunched over the bar, the unsteadiness of his gaze. It may be early, but the man had clearly already had a few. Just as clearly he was in the mood to talk. Matt wasn't about to rebuff the friendliest greeting he'd gotten yet in this town.

"Yes, I am," Matt said easily. "Just got in today."

"And leavin' today, too, I reckon," the man cackled, laughing at his own apparent joke.

"What makes you say that?" Matt asked.

"Not much to see around here. Why would anybody stick around?"

"Looks like I'll be here for a while, actually. Just took a job. The Weston Ranch."

Out of the corner of his eye, Matt saw the bartender, who'd started back with his beer, suddenly stop. The drunk's eyebrows shot upward. He stared blearily at Matt for a few long seconds before reaching for his own drink.

"Might not be around as long as you think," the man said into his glass.

"Why's that?"

The bartender dropped Matt's beer down on the

counter in front of him so hard some of it sloshed over the sides of the glass. He made no move to wipe it up. "Woman you're working for's probably going to be in jail soon."

Matt met the man's steady gaze and returned it. He had no intention of being intimidated by the bartender any more than he had been by the deputy. The sooner word got out that he wasn't going to be a pushover, the better.

But the longer he held the man's eyes, the more Matt registered that what he saw in them wasn't anger or hostility. Just a cold matter-of-factness that somehow was even more disturbing.

If that was the man's attitude toward Elena, Matt really didn't feel like throwing a big tip his way. Not to mention he had the feeling now that not even a tip could get the bartender to open up. His new friend a couple stools down, on the other hand, seemed like someone he'd like to keep talking.

Matt set the twenty down on the bar. "Bring my friend here another," he said, nodding to the other man.

His lips thinning, the bartender took the bill and moved away again.

"Why, thank you," the drunk said, tipping his almost empty glass in Matt's direction. "Name's Roy Fuller."

"Matt Alvarez."

"See, Ben," Fuller said to the bartender. "He's not a bad sort. Besides, he's new. Might not even know about Bobby."

"If you mean the murder, I know," Matt said. "I met a local deputy. He tried to scare me off."

The drunk nodded so hard Matt almost expected his head to pop off his neck. "That'd be Travis. He and

Bobby were tight. Always were since they were kids. He's got to be taking this real personal."

That was putting it mildly. "That makes sense the way he was acting," Matt agreed.

"Yeah, Travis always did have a temper, and Bobby was like a brother to him. Not to mention he never did like Elena. He's got to be coming for her hard. Hell, most folks are. Bobby was the last of the Westons. That means something around here."

The bartender set the new beer in front of Fuller, who reached for it greedily.

"A family that important must have had some enemies," Matt suggested.

"You'd think so, wouldn't you? But no, not Bobby. He was a good one."

"*Everybody* has enemies," Matt pressed. "There wasn't anybody who had a problem with him?"

"Only that wife of his," Fuller snickered. "Why do you think she killed him?"

His words drew Matt up short. "You think she did it?"

"Of course. Folks liked Bobby. Nobody had a reason to want him dead. Nobody but her."

Matt felt his heart sink. Staring into the man's bleary gaze, Matt knew he wasn't lying or putting on an act. Fuller really did believe Elena killed her husband.

He glanced at the bartender to find him staring at him. The man nodded, the gesture seeming to say "I told you so."

"I heard he was having money problems," Matt said.

"Times are rough for everybody. Only person who cared about his money problems was his wife, who didn't want him spending any. He was always wanting to make changes and improvements on the ranch and she was always fighting him. Can't blame her, I suppose. Elena grew up poor, never had much. Makes sense she'd be tight with money." Fuller shot him a look. "I hope she's paying you well enough, especially since people might be giving you trouble for working for her."

"So he wasn't in debt to anybody?" Money could be a strong motive for murder.

"Not that I heard."

Which didn't necessarily mean anything. A lot of people kept money matters private. If Weston had been in trouble with someone, it was possible no one knew but him and the other person.

Matt wanted to believe he wasn't just clutching at straws. He couldn't quite manage it.

He tried to think of something else he could ask, another possibility he could pursue, but came up empty. Which wasn't good. Despite what Elena had told him, he'd figured there had to be someone out there who had a known beef with Bobby, maybe one she didn't know about if they were as estranged as she said. He'd meant what he'd said. Everybody had enemies. Heck, Elena seemed to have nothing but in this town.

Elena...

He frowned as a fresh thought occurred to him. Maybe he was just looking at this all wrong. Bobby Weston may not have had any enemies—though he still doubted that—but maybe this wasn't about him. Maybe it was about someone who did have plenty of people against her.

Elena.

Bobby Weston might be dead, but she was the one in a lot of trouble. Could all of this somehow be about *her?*

"Tell me more about this woman who hired me," he said to Fuller. "What's so bad about her?"

A laugh burst out of Fuller's mouth. "Killing her husband isn't enough for you?"

"She hasn't been convicted yet," Matt pointed out. "She hasn't even been arrested and it's been a couple weeks, so there must not be much real evidence against her. But it seems like the whole town's ready to believe she's guilty." He sent a pointed look the bartender's way, only to get the same stony stare in return. "And you said the deputy never liked her to begin with. She's got to be a pretty terrible person for everybody to turn on her like that."

Fuller waved a hand dismissively. "Eh, I never had a problem with her. Her mother took off and her father was a bum, but she was an okay kid. Not popular or anything. Quiet, kept to herself. One of those kids you could tell was dreaming of getting out of here."

"So why don't people like her?"

"I think it was mostly marrying Weston that did it. That's when people started looking at her different, and not in a good way. Before, they ignored her. After, they couldn't. Weston was too big around here, too much a part of the town. That made her part of the town, and people didn't like that. She wasn't in her place. Really it all comes back to the money again. Everybody knew that was why she'd married him. She was dirt poor with a bum for a father, and she ended up hitched to the biggest name in this town. People judged her for that, especially after they saw her and Bobby weren't really happy. They blamed her for that, for not making him happy. So when he turned up dead, nobody was surprised she killed him. She was in it for the money, and she finally killed him for it."

Matt let the man's words sink in. He had to admit it made sense—not her killing Weston, of course, but the reasons for the marriage and why the town had turned on her. He knew more than anybody how much security had meant to her back then. She'd married a guy who could give her that, so if it wasn't for the money itself, it was for what the money could provide. Why else would she marry him so fast, after only three months? She'd known Matt that long, and sure as hell hadn't chosen him.

The only other explanation he could think of was that she really had loved Weston—far more than she'd loved Matt, than he'd loved her.

He wasn't sure which answer he'd like less.

He was crazy about me, and I...was crazy about him.

A sharp pain shafted through him at the idea. Which was just stupid, he thought angrily, trying to shake off the feeling. It was the past. It had been eight years. He was over it, over her. There was no reason it should hurt to know she hadn't loved him as much as he'd thought he loved her.

But even as he thought it, the burn of that pain he'd felt in response lingered, too sharp to be shaken off that easily. He didn't even want to think about why that was.

"Hey, don't take it so hard," Fuller said, likely misreading whatever was on Matt's face. "I say go on and work for her. How many people like who they have to work for, you know? Unlike Ben here—" he raised his glass to the bartender "—I don't begrudge you the work. Times like these, a man's gotta do what he has to.

But don't get too comfortable, I'll tell you that. And you might want to get her to pay you up front. Fact is, your new boss is headed to jail. It's only a matter of time."

Chapter Six

For the first time in more than a week, when Elena heard the sound of someone pulling into the driveway, her heart didn't sink with dread. Instead, she felt a rush of anticipation, the feeling racing through her.

Then she realized the cause, the knowledge turning the small smile that had formed on her lips into a frown.

Matt. She was excited because Matt was back.

She shook herself. Good God, what was she doing?

Her husband had been dead for little more than a week. It hardly mattered that the feelings she'd once had for him had long since died. She had no business feeling this way about anyone right now, certainly not a man who'd suddenly reappeared in her life after eight years.

Nostalgia, she told herself. What she was experiencing was just the effect of old memories. Which made even less sense considering how everything had ended between them.

The reminder should have been enough to kill the ridiculous emotional response. Still, she had to squelch another little tremor of anticipation as she made her way out of the barn where she'd been giving the horses their feed.

But when she reached the barn door, she saw it

wasn't Matt's truck sitting in the driveway. Glen Marshall stood on the front porch.

Disappointment welled in her chest, the feeling just as absurd as the excitement she'd felt moments earlier. She tried to shake it off and forced a smile as she made her way up to the house. "Evening, Glen," she called when she was close enough.

He matched her smile. "Evening, Elena. Is this a good time to stop by?"

His smile was as warm as it had always been, and she felt another twinge of guilt for the disappointment she'd felt when she'd seen it was him. A hearty man in his fifties, Glen was a successful rancher and had been a close friend of the Westons for years. More important, he was just about the only person in the area who didn't treat her like an outcast. If anything, she should be glad to see his friendly face.

"Of course," she said, crossing the porch and pushing the door open. "Come on in."

Pulling his hat from his head, he stepped over the threshold and past her into the house. Elena closed the door behind him and nodded toward the living room. "Have a seat."

"Thank you." He took the chair on the far side of the coffee table, Elena taking the one opposite. "I heard you had some trouble in town today," he said with an almost convincing casualness.

"I'm sure you did. And I bet whoever shared that news with you sounded pretty pleased, didn't they?"

He had the grace to look away, but she could tell from the way he hesitated before answering that she was right.

"I wanted to make sure you were all right, and also talk to you about something."

"I'm fine," she said. "Already got my truck fixed and safely home, good as new. What did you want to talk to me about?"

"I'm sure Bobby probably mentioned that I'd offered to buy the ranch from him recently."

Elena nodded. "He did." And had been none too pleased about it. Glen and Big Jim Weston had been good friends ever since they were boys. After Big Jim's death, Glen had sort of offered himself as a surrogate father to Bobby and his brother Junior, especially when it came to ranching matters. He'd been there to guide Junior, and then Bobby, giving advice when it was asked for and a willing ear when needed. Bobby had taken Glen's offer as a sign the man didn't have faith in him and didn't think he could handle the ranch. Elena wasn't so sure that wasn't exactly the case. If anyone besides her had known how much Bobby had been struggling to keep things going around here, it was Glen. The fact that he'd thrown Bobby a lifeline when he needed one so badly probably wasn't a coincidence.

"I want to make the same offer to you, with the same terms, though I'm certainly open to negotiation."

The offer was a good one. More than good, really. Certainly more than the ranch would fetch on the open market in this economy. She'd wanted Bobby to take it. Of course, he hadn't. "I appreciate that. I'll definitely give it some thought."

She could tell it wasn't the answer he'd been looking for and suspected he'd thought she'd say yes right away. "Can I be completely honest with you, Elena?"

"I hope you will be."

"Look, I don't think there's any question a lot of people think you killed Bobby. Not me," he said quickly, "but a lot of people. And certainly Walt."

"True enough."

"Have you thought about hiring a lawyer?"

"Unfortunately, I have," she admitted. "If Walt and Travis have their way, I'm going to need one sometime soon. I just don't know how I'm going to pay for one."

"I figured as much. Which is another reason I thought I should reiterate my offer. If you sell now, you can use the funds from the sale to buy the best lawyer money can buy, not have to worry about that."

She couldn't argue with him. The longer the threat of an arrest loomed over her head, she'd wondered how she was going to pay for an attorney should the time come. And even without lawyer fees to pay, she could use the money. Even so…

"Thank you for your concern, but I think it's too early to consider making any kind of deal. I haven't even had a chance to deal with Bobby's will."

"I understand that. So I thought I'd let you know I would be willing to make an advance payment once the papers are signed. You could use the money right away."

The new twist drew her up short and actually made her consider it for a moment. He was certainly being more than generous. But even if she was ready to make a deal, she couldn't even afford a lawyer to handle that for her.

"I really do appreciate the offer, Glen, but I have to admit I feel a little like I'd be taking advantage of you. We both know the land's not worth as much as you're proposing."

"It is to me," he said. "The Westons have always

meant a great deal to me, and I'd hate to see the land they worked for generations sold to just anybody."

It was the same thing he'd told Bobby, and she knew it was true. "I understand, but with everything that's going on right now, I'm really not ready to face selling the ranch at the moment. But if and when the time comes I can sell, you can be sure I'll think of you first."

Again, she got the sense he was disappointed. She was almost afraid he would try to pressure her further, but instead he simply nodded. "I appreciate that."

She did her best not to let her relief show that he was letting the subject go for now. She knew his intentions were good, and she would certainly be hard-pressed to find a better offer, but this was the last thing she wanted to think about today.

The sound of a vehicle approaching outside met her ears. This time there was no rush of anticipation. There was no telling who it might be.

Glen glanced at her. "Expecting company?"

"It might be the new hand I hired to help out around here. He should be getting back from town."

She saw Glen's eyebrows rise in surprise. Before he could say anything, she quickly rose to her feet. He followed suit a moment later.

Together they walked to the front door, reaching the porch in time to see Matt climbing out of his truck.

"I didn't know you were looking for new hands, Elena," Glen said, in a tone she couldn't quite read.

"I wasn't," she said. "I needed to, but obviously I've had other things on my mind."

Before he closed the truck door, Matt's attention zeroed in on her and Glen. As he made his way to the porch, his gaze shifted from her to Glen and back. She read the question in his eyes, as though seeking a signal from her whether the man was friend or foe.

"Glen, this is Matt Alvarez," she said easily. "Matt, Glen Marshall, a good friend of my husband's family."

Glen shot her a quick look. "*Your* family, Elena."

She forced a small smile. "Of course." Glen might consider her a Weston, but if so, he was likely the only one around here who ever had.

"Well, I should be going," Glen said. "But again, think about my offer. I don't think you'll get a better one."

"I will," she promised again.

With a nod to Matt, Glen headed back to his truck. Matt and Elena watched him go in silence.

"Everything go okay in town?" she asked when Glen began to back out of the driveway.

"No problems. What offer?"

"To buy the ranch," she explained. "It was a standing offer he had with Bobby. He wanted me to know it's still on the table." She shook her head. "Not that it matters at the moment. I'm in no position to sell anyway. I haven't even been able to talk to Bobby's lawyer about his will."

"Why not?"

"Mostly because his lawyer seems to be avoiding me," she acknowledged with more than a little irritation. "Not that I'm surprised."

"What do you mean?"

"Jack Landry is the executor of Bobby's estate, not to mention the only lawyer in town. He also happens to be Bobby's cousin."

"I thought Bobby was the last of the Westons."

"He is. Jack's not a Weston. His mother and Bobby's were sisters."

"So he's probably not happy about the idea of you inheriting."

"Nope. I made a couple calls to his office, and was told he wasn't available. I left messages both times, and he hasn't returned them. With everything else that's been going on, I haven't had time to follow up further yet. And to be honest, I started to worry how bad it would look if it seemed like I was too eager to see what I'd inherited from Bobby. Everybody already thinks I killed him. I didn't want to give them any more reason to think so at the moment."

"You think this Jack Landry believes you're guilty, too, and that's why he's putting you off?"

"Probably. Most people figure my arrest is only a matter of time." Elena shot him a wry look. "Glen pointed out I could probably use the money for my up-coming defense, should I need it. He even offered to advance me the money from the sale."

"Nice of him," Matt noted drily. "Sounds like he wants the ranch pretty bad. He wanted to buy it when Bobby was alive?"

"Yeah. He made a very generous offer, too."

"Hmm. You ever wonder just how badly he wants it?"

"What do you mean?"

He looked at her with the utmost seriousness. "Badly enough to kill for it?"

Elena simply shook her head. "Hardly. Glen has his own spread. The Weston ranch is smaller than Glen's and isn't even adjacent so it's not as though he could combine them. Bobby's brother, Junior, was Glen's godson, and he and Bobby were about as close. He's just a family friend trying to do a good deed for a family he was close to for years and cared about deeply. The offer really is just a gesture of pity, something Bobby knew full well, which is another reason he refused to sell."

"Are you sure about that? There couldn't be some other reason he wants the ranch?"

"Like what?"

"I don't know. That doesn't mean there isn't one, something you don't know about. Something that could be a motive. Are you really considering his offer?"

"I'd be a fool not to. It's a much better one than I'm likely to get from anyone else, certainly more than I'd get on the open market."

"And that doesn't make you suspicious?"

"I suppose it should." Elena exhaled sharply. He was right. As she'd told him, her first instinct was to believe no one had a motive to kill Bobby, yet clearly someone had, so she must be missing something. Could Glen really want the ranch so badly that he was willing to kill Bobby to get it for some reason she wasn't aware of yet? "And here I thought no one had any motives."

"Maybe you just needed a fresh set of eyes, somebody who doesn't know these people to look at them with a different perspective."

Someone who was inclined not to trust easily? Knowing what she did about his life history, she supposed this came naturally to him, not trusting people. The idea made her sad, but at the moment maybe that quality was exactly what she needed in her life.

"I guess it's a good thing you're here, then," she said softly. Even to her own ears the words sounded far more weighted with meaning and full of feeling than she'd intended.

His eyes went dark with some unreadable emotion, his expression enigmatic.

"Maybe it is," he agreed.

Chapter Seven

She ran as hard and fast as her body could manage, her lungs heaving, her legs pumping wildly, the pavement hard beneath her feet. And still it wasn't fast enough. She pushed her body harder, fear and adrenaline and pure desperation pounding through her veins. She had to get there sooner.

She had to get to him.

And then there he was, leaning against the truck he'd parked in the shadows at the edge of Main Street, barely out of reach of the nearest streetlight. It was their spot, the one where he'd met her that first night and all those nights after. It was as private a spot as the town had to offer, the rest of the street quiet and deserted at this time of night. She didn't have time to feel relief or take a breath. At the sight of him, she picked up a fresh burst of speed she wouldn't have thought herself capable of and ran even faster, hurtling toward him in the dark.

She saw the moment he spotted her, pushing himself away from the truck and moving forward to meet her, clearly as unable to wait for her as she was for him. The moonlight lit his face. It almost didn't seem necessary with the happiness radiating from his expression, the smile beaming on his lips. She immediately smiled, too, joy bursting within her. And when she launched herself at him, he was there to catch her, his arms wide and strong and open, closing around her and holding her tight.

"Elena," he breathed against her hair, the sound of his voice sending warmth rolling through her like a soft caress.

"Matt." There was so much more she wanted to say, but that single word—his name—was all she could manage to get out past the lump in her throat. And suddenly she realized she was crying, hot tears burning her eyes.

"What's wrong?" he whispered gently.

"I was just so scared I'd never see you again." Never look at his beautiful face. Never hear his voice. Never touch him. Never feel his arms around her.

He said nothing, only tightened his hold and held her even closer. It was answer enough that he'd felt the same way.

Finally, needing to see him, needing to say all those words she had inside, she pulled back to peer up into his face. "I'm so sorry. It's not right. It's not fair."

One corner of his mouth curved wryly. "Hey, can't say you didn't warn me. Your dad did go crazy."

Yes, he had, she thought, fresh anger surging inside her. There'd been times over the past several months when Matt had questioned whether it was really necessary for them to be so secretive. She herself had sometimes felt foolish about it. She was an adult, should probably be past the age when she should care about her father's reaction to her love life. Except Ed's re-

sponse when he'd learned about them had proven just how right she'd been to be worried.

He'd acted like a complete lunatic, ranting and raving to anyone who'd listen—whether they wanted to or not. He'd made a fool of himself, but he'd also accomplished exactly what he'd wanted—gotten Matt fired, ensured there was no longer a place for him in Western Bluff, so he'd have no choice but to move on.

She shuddered, fear striking directly at her heart.

"At least I know you weren't trying to hide me because you were ashamed of me or something," Matt said. The words were dry, laconic, but she knew him well enough to know the genuine fear he must have felt deep down, even if he'd never admit it consciously, even to himself. He'd been hurt too deeply, rejected too much by those who should have loved him the most, not to guard himself against the possibility of it happening again.

"Never," she said firmly, fiercely, meaning it as much as anything she'd ever said in her life. How could she ever be ashamed of him? He was the best man she'd ever known. It seemed impossible that they'd only known each other for three months. She couldn't imagine living without him.

Which brought them to this.

A sudden chill rolled through her. "So what happens now?" she made herself ask.

"I have to go," he said quietly.

She lowered her head and nodded faintly. Of course. She knew it was true. She just hadn't wanted to think about what it meant for them. She would be leaving soon enough herself, but she would be going back to school. And he... "Where will you go?"

"I don't know. Wherever I can get a job. It might take some time, but I saved up enough this summer to get by for a while until I find something. Hopefully it won't take too long."

A hesitant note entered his final words, betraying his uncertainty. Of course, he had to do whatever he could to find work. And the longer it took, the greater the likelihood the search would take him farther and farther away.

Far from here. Far from her.

His hands suddenly tightened on her arms.

"Come with me."

She raised her head, her heart racing, pounding, threatening to burst through her chest.

"Where?"

"Wherever I go," he said immediately. "I don't know where I'm heading. But I need you with me." He swallowed, and the flash of vulnerability on his masculine face made her heart twist painfully.

"I love you."

It wasn't the first time he'd told her that but it might as well have been from the rush of giddiness that soared through her, filling her with so much sheer happiness it didn't seem possible her body, her heart, her soul could contain it. And in that moment, she would have agreed to anything he said. Of course she would go with him. She would follow him to the ends of the earth and they would be together. Because he loved her. And she loved him. And that was all that mattered. Nothing else possibly could.

Nothing.

Except it did.

Like an insidious whisper, the thought slid through

her, a chill washing over her and extinguishing her joy as the full implications of his words settled in.

The image of him on the open road, traveling, looking for work, rose again in her mind. But this time she saw herself there with him. The uncertainty. The fear of not knowing what would happen or how they'd pay the bills, where the next paycheck would come from.

It was a life she knew too well. That was what it was like growing up with her father, the uncertainty, the precariousness. She couldn't live like that anymore. That was why she'd always been determined to get out of this town, to go to college.

College, where she was supposed to return in just a few weeks.

College, which she'd been working toward her whole life, which offered the promise of stability and certainty she'd craved and desperately wanted—needed—for so long.

How could she give up that bright future, all her hopes and dreams, to follow him into the dark unknown?

As fear gripped her insides, clenching her stomach, closing off her breath, she knew the answer without a doubt.

She couldn't.

But he loves me.

Yes, she thought, peering up into his dark eyes. She didn't doubt that. But she felt none of that love. She only felt fear.

He was still looking down at her, his face aglow, as though certain what she would say, as certain as she'd been only moments ago.

And she realized it had only been a few moments

since he'd made the offer. She felt so cold inside it was hard to believe she'd ever been happy and warm, let alone mere moments ago.

Still he waited for her answer, not yet realizing anything was wrong.

There was only one answer she could give.

"I can't."

He blinked, no other reaction on his face, as though the words hadn't had any impact.

"What do you mean?"

"I can't go with you."

He finally frowned, eyebrows furrowing in confusion. "Why not?"

"I have to go back to school. It's my future. It's everything I've been working toward for years." She almost winced. The words were all true, but they sounded so hollow spoken aloud compared to how they had in her head.

"You can have a future with me."

Again the words inspired a rush of emotion, of pure longing, at the possibilities they offered.

But then she remembered the costs. "Doing what? Going from town to town? Getting work on a ranch, too?"

"You've been waiting tables," he pointed out.

"For the summer! I don't want to do it forever. I want something more than that. I need to go to school." Suddenly inspiration struck, fresh hope flaring inside her. "You can come back to Austin with me when I go back to school." The idea was so perfect she could barely contain her excitement at hearing it voiced aloud.

His frown merely deepened. "And do what? Hang around while you go to school?"

"You can get a job."

"Doing what? Ranch work is all I've ever done. It's all I know. And I don't want to live in the city. I could never be happy in a place like that."

"Even if I'm there?"

His voice softened the slightest bit, but his expression was unyielding. "Even then."

"How do you know if you haven't tried?"

"I know," he said firmly. "How do you know you won't be happy on a ranch with me?"

"It's just not the life I want."

His expression hardened. "Or maybe I'm not what you want."

"You are!" she said without hesitation.

"Well, if you loved me, you would come with me."

"If you loved *me, you would come with me."*

"I can't," he said dully.

"Well, I can't, either."

He stared at her, and though he hadn't moved a muscle and his expression didn't change she could feel him slipping away from her. She almost reached out to grab on to him and hold him to her.

Before she could, he took another, inexorable step back. "Then I guess there's nothing left to say."

She wanted to argue. There was obviously so much to say. But as she stared into his eyes, panic gripping her throat, she knew there was nothing she could do. Nothing but to take it back and say she'd go with him. It was the only thing that could possibly dim the raw fury in his eyes.

But it wasn't the anger that made her heart squeeze and her lungs feel like they were being pummeled. It was what she saw beneath it. The hurt, the sheer agony.

*And she knew she'd wounded him, just as she knew
why. At least why it had to seem that way from his
point of view.*

*But he was wrong. He had to see this was different.
This wasn't like his mother, or his father or any of the
other people in his life who'd rejected him and hadn't
wanted him. That wasn't what she was doing.*

*Before she could begin to summon the words to deny
it, he turned and walked away.*

*She watched him storm to his truck, his boots kick-
ing up dirt with each angry step. The whole time she
waited for him to stop and turn back, expecting it,
knowing it would happen. It couldn't end like this. He
couldn't just leave her. It wasn't possible.*

*The engine started with a roar. Seemingly a split
second later, the truck began to back up, quickly turning and shooting out onto the road.*

She stood there, her throat frozen in shock.

He'll come back. He'll come back. He has to.

*She watched as the truck peeled away in the night,
growing smaller, the taillights fading, until the tears
finally blurred her sight and she could see nothing at
all, the thought still echoing in her mind.*

He'll come back.

He has to.

He'll come back…

ELENA BOLTED UPRIGHT IN BED, her heart pounding, her
lungs squeezing so painfully she couldn't breathe. She
leaned forward, desperately trying to pull in air. It felt
as if she was being suffocated, as though she were
dying.

Until she realized she *was* breathing, her chest falling up and down, the breath flowing into and out of her lungs. But it didn't ease the agony she felt in her chest, the sense that she was dying. And she realized it had nothing to do with not being able to breathe.

No, she remembered the feeling well, even without having dreamed it again. It was the feeling of having her heart broken, the worst experience of her life, the most painful thing she'd ever been through.

She sat there, trying to shake the awful feeling that continued to grip her. She began to push her hair back, only to realize the wetness she felt on her cheeks wasn't the remembered sensation of the dream. She brushed her fingers across her face to find it damp with tears. Damn. She hadn't had the dream in years, but it was as real to her as ever.

Those words continued to echo in her ears as loudly as though they'd actually been spoken an instant before.

He'll come back.

Except he hadn't. As long as she'd waited that warm summer night and the days and months that followed, Matt never had come back.

No, she realized with a start. It was different this time. Because after all these years, the dream had a different ending in reality.

He *had* come back.

And then her heart was beating faster again. It was eight years later, so much had happened—*was* happening—and it was nothing like she'd once imagined, but he was here.

He'd come back.

She sat there, trying to adjust to that basic fact that changed so much. It had been years since she'd had the dream, and it had returned only when the reality had changed.

He was here, in the bunkhouse just a short distance from where she lay.

Then she heard it.

A sound. A thump. Coming from somewhere outside.

Somewhere downstairs.

And for the first time it struck her that she hadn't simply woken from the dream.

No, something had woken her.

She quickly jumped from the bed, reaching for the gun she'd placed on the bedside table for safety's sake. From the moment she'd found Bobby dead downstairs, she hadn't felt completely safe in this house. The gun didn't do a lot to reassure her, but at least it was something. At the moment, she couldn't have been happier to have it there.

Matt was nearby, in the bunkhouse. He might as well have been a million miles away for all the good he could do her there. If there was trouble, it was here.

Or did he already know? He'd said he would try to keep an eye out overnight. At the time she'd appreciated the gesture, but thought he was being overly cautious. True, she was uneasy in the house, but deep down she didn't believe the killer was coming back. And while people in town were giving her a cold shoulder, she didn't see them coming after her out here. Of course, no one had slashed her tires before, either. She probably shouldn't count anything out at this point.

Moving to the window, she peered out.

She didn't see anything, but that didn't mean nothing was there.

A shadow suddenly shifted at the edge of the yard. Her heart jumping, she whipped her head toward it.

Just in time to see Matt step into the light.

Relief shuddered from her lungs and she relaxed slightly. Then she noticed he was armed, too, a gun lowered but held in his right hand. He stepped forward gradually, cautiously, slowly looking from side to side as he moved toward the house.

Elena automatically shoved away from the window and headed for the door.

She raced downstairs. Seconds later, she was at the front door. Quickly checking outside before opening it, she spotted Matt just reaching the front steps. He was frowning. He still didn't have his gun raised and didn't seem particularly concerned. No, he seemed angry.

Something had definitely happened.

Figuring it was safe enough and needing to know what it was, she pulled the door open and stepped out on the porch.

He drew to a halt at the sight of her, surprise flashing across his face.

"What is it?" she asked. "What happened?"

Matt stood there, staring at her with a distinct sense of unease, his mouth slightly open.

"What?" she demanded, unable to take the suspense.

"Elena—" Shoving his gun into the back of his waistband, he stepped onto the porch, then stopped again and swallowed, his eyes flicking over her shoulder for an instant. Just a tiny gesture, little more than a reflex.

And a telling one. It was enough. Curious, she turned around.

Then she finally saw them, the letters spray painted

in bright red on the front of the house to the left of the door.

She stepped back, partly from surprise, partly from revulsion, unable to escape the word the huge letters spelled out on the wall in such a garish tone.

MURDERER.

She flinched, the ugliness of it striking her like a punch to the face. It was all so ugly. There was no other word for it. The word itself. The garish red paint. The sentiment behind it. The fact that someone had come here, to her home, the one place in this world she should be safe, in the middle of the night and defaced it out of their hatred for her.

She dropped her head, unable to stand looking at it anymore, but unable to force her body into motion to turn away.

She sensed him come up behind her, approaching slowly, coming close enough that she could feel him there behind her.

"Hey," he said. "It's going to be okay."

"Is it?" she responded automatically, hating the quiver she heard in her own voice.

"Yes," he said firmly, his voice pulsing with anger. "They're not going to get away with this. I'm not going to let them."

Every word rang with certainty and determination, leaving her no doubt he fully intended to do what he promised. She just wasn't sure if even he was capable of it.

Them. It didn't matter if it was only one person who had done this. Because it wasn't just one person against her. It was the whole town.

This damn town. She should have gotten out when

she'd had the chance, should have left it behind her and never looked back.

Should have left with him...

Matt gently turned her around to face him, his hands laying lightly on her upper arms. "Hey," he said again. "Don't let them do this to you. You're going to make it through this."

It was the tenderness in his voice more than the words alone that called to her, making her raise her head to meet his eyes.

The kindness she saw there, the concern, nearly broke her. She couldn't even remember the last time anyone had looked at her like that, when anyone had so simply and genuinely cared about her feelings. To have it come from this man, a man she'd once believed she loved, a man she hadn't thought she'd ever see again just twenty-four hours ago, was almost more than she could bear.

She stared up into his eyes, this man who'd been out of her life for eight long years, who'd reappeared in her life so suddenly for reasons she still wasn't sure she understood, or maybe wasn't sure she believed. Once again she found herself studying him, trying to understand what he was thinking, what he was doing here. At least at first. Because, as it always had before, the longer she looked the more it struck her how beautiful he was. His face was more mature, even more masculine than before, and somehow even more beautiful.

Then she saw that look in his eyes change, becoming more heated, more intense, stroking over her face.

And out of nowhere, she felt her body respond. The emotions that had been churning within her ebbed away, replaced by an incredible sense of warmth that built from her core, pooling in her belly and flowing outward to fill every part of her.

She'd tried to tell herself that what she was feeling was the residual emotions from her memories. She wasn't really this attracted to him now.

But this wasn't nostalgia. This wasn't a remembered emotion. It was real, and it was more powerful than anything she remembered.

It was also madness. He'd been back in her life less than a day.

It didn't matter that her marriage had died long before her husband did. Bobby had been dead for less than two weeks. To feel something for someone else so soon, especially *this* someone else…

Would be a mistake, she reminded herself firmly. And she'd already made far too many of those in her life.

She deliberately took a step back, breaking the eye contact to glance down the empty driveway. "Did you see them?" she made herself ask. "Did you see who did this?"

"No," he said, turning to follow her gaze. "I'm sorry."

"It's okay. They must have come on foot. If they'd driven up we would have heard them." She frowned. "Though I did think I heard something…"

"An engine?"

"No, some kind of noise. That's why I got up. I thought I heard something outside the house."

Their eyes met, and she saw him coming to the same conclusion she was. If the noise had been made by the vandal responsible for this, then that person had been around not too long ago.

Could still be somewhere nearby now.

"Stay here," he ordered. Without waiting for a response, he bounded back down the stairs, grabbing his gun from the back of his waistband. Checking in both directions, he tore off around the back of the house to the left.

Suddenly realizing she still had her own weapon in hand, Elena raised it and held it poised in front of her. She scanned the yard and driveway for any signs of anyone. Logic said whoever had done this had probably taken off as soon as they'd completed what they'd come here for, not wanting to get caught. But part of her wondered if they might not have lingered, wanting to see her reaction, the result of their handiwork.

And she'd given them exactly what they most likely wanted, she realized, remembering her reaction, the way her first glimpse of the vandalism had hit her. She was instantly angry, as much with herself as with the person who'd defaced her home. She could just imagine that person standing out there in the dark, waiting to see how she reacted, relishing in having been able to torment her.

No more.

She didn't know if they were still out there—she doubted it—but she still straightened her spine and stared out into the darkness. She hoped they were watching.

Because she'd had enough. She wasn't going to put up with any more, and she'd be damned if she let anyone in this town see a hint of weakness from her again.

Chapter Eight

It was almost noon when Matt got up the next day. As soon as he saw the time, he felt guilty for having slept in, rising to his feet with a muffled curse. He'd intended to get up early and check on the horses and maybe the cattle, familiarize himself with the way things were around here. Elena had shown him around a bit last night after dinner, but he wanted to get a feel for the place on his own. If the two of them were going to keep this place running by themselves, they were going to have to figure out how to make it work.

Then again, there were more important things to focus on, and it wasn't like he'd gotten much sleep last night. He'd run around in the dark for what seemed like hours. There'd been no trace of the scumbag who'd vandalized Elena's house. As far as Matt could tell, the guy had most likely parked on the main road and walked up, approaching from the side. It wasn't that long of a walk, there weren't any lights along that way to reveal an intruder, and someone could likely get in and out pretty easily.

The guy might not know it, but he should really consider himself lucky for having gotten away. He probably wouldn't have liked what would have happened if

Matt had gotten his hands on him, not after he'd seen the look the bastard's actions had put in Elena's eyes.

He still might not, Matt amended. Somebody who'd pulled something like that once might be willing to try it again, and Matt had no intention of letting him get away twice.

In the meantime, there was ranch business to be taken care of, not to mention a murder investigation to deal with. Far too much for him to spend any more time in bed.

He showered and dressed quickly, intending to check on Elena first thing. She'd looked calmer, stronger, *angrier* when they'd met back up after his unsuccessful search for the intruder. He'd been glad to see her resilience in action, but he still remembered how shattered she'd looked when he'd been unable to keep her from seeing what the intruder had painted on the house, how lost.

And how beautiful, staring up at him in the moonlight.

Yes, he remembered that, too. It was just something else he didn't have time to deal with right now.

He was pulling his boots on when his cell phone rang.

Recognizing the number, he quickly answered. "This is Matt."

"It's Pam," she said shortly.

"Glad to hear from you," he said, meaning it. They really could use any help she had to give. "What do you have for me?"

"Not much on the town. It seems like a pretty typical small town without much to distinguish it. A fairly insular, static community. Not many people move there or leave. It generally hasn't made the news, barely makes the map."

Yeah, sounded like Western Bluff all right. "What about Elena and her husband?"

"Elena Reyes, born twenty-eight years ago. Robert Weston, born thirty years ago, died thirteen days ago. Both natives of Western Bluff. She graduated from UT, he went to Rice. They married at the county courthouse there seven years ago. Still married at the time of his death."

"What was their financial situation like?"

"Not great. The Weston ranch is heavily mortgaged and they're carrying a lot of debt."

So it was as Elena had said. "And the sheriff?"

"Walter 'Walt' Bremer was elected sheriff six years ago. He seems competent enough at his job. He's received the usual commendations from local and state law enforcement. Then again, his job usually doesn't involve investigating murders. There has been exactly one in his jurisdiction since he became sheriff."

Even if the sheriff had years investigating homicides under his belt, Matt wasn't sure he'd trust him to investigate this one.

It was all important information to have, but he wasn't sure what good it did him. Problem was he wasn't sure what else he needed to know. "Anything else?"

"Well, there is one thing I found interesting, though I can't say if you'll agree. Western Bluff did pop up on the Bureau's radar once a while back. A number of women were reported missing in the area over a seven-year span between twenty to twenty-seven years ago. Western Bluff was pretty much in the center of the reported disappearances, and there wasn't much else out there, so the investigation kind of focused on the town for a while. What really got someone's attention is that all the women matched the same general profile, Hispanic women in their twenties or early thirties. They were considering that the disappearances were connected, maybe a serial killer was operating in the area. Nothing much came of it, though. They were never able to prove that anything happened to any of the women. Some of them were Mexican nationals who might have just gone home."

Matt frowned. Twenty-five years ago one particular Latino woman had disappeared from the area, a woman who must have been in her twenties or early thirties when she apparently left town.

It was probably a coincidence, but at the same time, he couldn't help but wonder where Teresa Reyes had ended up. If anything, Elena might like to know, although there was no guarantee a happy reunion would be at the end, he thought, remembering his meeting with his father.

Still, he had to ask. "Can you see if you can find anything on Elena's mother? I believe her name is Teresa, Teresa Reyes. She left Elena's father twenty-five years ago. At least that's what everyone thinks."

"You think something else might have happened to her?"

"I don't know. But I'd be interested to know where she is now."

"I'll see what I can find."

"One more thing. Can you get me a list of possible criminal defense attorneys in the area, or maybe in all of Texas, who are damn good at their jobs?"

"You think an arrest is coming?"

"I don't know, but I want to be ready if it does."

"Sure thing."

"Thanks, Pam. I really appreciate it."

"You got it."

Matt was just about to shove the phone in his pocket when he spotted movement out of the corner of his eye. He whirled around to find a man standing inside the door, eyeing Matt warily.

"Who are you?" the man demanded.

He had some nerve, Matt had to give him that. "Somebody who's supposed to be here, unlike you. So I'm the one who's going to be asking the questions. Who are *you?*"

The man's lips thinned with anger, and Matt wasn't sure at first he was going to answer. "Carter Baines," he finally said. "I used to work here."

"*Used* to. You don't now, so you have no business being here."

"I lived here for years. Think I left something behind and came back for it."

"What is it?"

"My business, not yours."

"It is as long as *I'm* the one living here now. Either way, this isn't your property."

"I just wanted what was mine."

"You could have called Mrs. Weston and asked her to look for it."

The man's mouth curled in a sneer. "Had no interest in talking to *her.* If she was in jail where she belonged I could have been in and out of here without any of this hassle."

"You believe she killed her husband," Matt said, leaving it as a statement.

"Of course she did. Who else?"

"You tell me."

"Nobody," Baines spat. "She's the only one with any reason to kill him."

Matt figured that wasn't worth arguing. "If you worked here for years, you have to know Mrs. Weston pretty well. She really strike you as the murdering type?"

"She struck me as the greedy type, and there's no telling what somebody'll do for money."

"What made you think she was greedy?"

"Everybody knows she's the reason Bobby never had any money to spend around here. She was always on him about money, never wanting him to spend a dime. He should have had more men working this place, should have been making improvements around here, but he couldn't. Because she wanted all the money for herself."

Anyone could see Elena wasn't exactly living an extravagant lifestyle. "You really believe that?"

"Everybody knows it!"

"And where was she spending all this money?" Matt asked. "As far as I can tell she doesn't have any expensive clothes or jewelry. She doesn't have a fancy car, doesn't look like she travels much—"

"I don't know what she's doing with it," the man said. "All I know is it's all she cares about."

It didn't make much sense, but Matt was starting to figure Carter Baines wasn't the smartest guy around. There really wasn't any point trying to make him see logic. Matt didn't know why he was wasting his breath on the guy anyway.

He was about to throw Baines out when a woman's voice rang out. "What's going on here?"

Elena stood in the doorway. Her gaze slid between him and Baines, finally settling on the other man as her lips turned down in a frown. "Carter? What are you doing here?"

The man didn't answer immediately, his scowl deepening as he glared at her.

"Mr. Baines says he left something here," Matt answered for him. "He came to get it."

"You should have called," she told Baines. "I could have had whatever you left sent to you."

"Just wanted to get my stuff," he grumbled under his breath. "Easier to come and get it."

"Maybe," she said patiently. "But you don't work or live here anymore. That was your decision, which means you're no longer welcome on this property without my permission."

It didn't seem possible, but the man's eyes narrowed further, tight slits glittering malice. "Damn greedy bitch."

The bastard had barely gotten that last hateful word out before fury exploded in Matt's veins, instantly propelling him forward. "That's it. You're done here—"

Baines continued as though he wasn't even there, his focus solely on Elena. "Forget it, I don't need my stuff. Marshall hired me on, and he pays a hell of a lot better than Bobby ever could because of you."

Matt frowned, the comment drawing him up short. Glen Marshall, the rancher who'd made the offer on this place, had hired Baines? It didn't say much about his judgment, as far as Matt was concerned. Unless there was more to it....

"You finally got what you wanted," Baines continued. "Enjoy it while you can, because you're not gonna be able to when you're in jail where you belong."

Nearly on top of him, Matt reached for Baines's arm, ready to throw the man out on his ass. He opened his mouth to tell him off—

Elena spoke first, her tone steady, cold and unwaveringly calm. "I think it's time for you to leave."

For the first time, the man seemed to notice Matt's closeness, glancing up, his eyes flaring in surprise. He straightened his spine in an apparent attempt at dignity he didn't deserve. "I'm out of here," he said, as if he had a choice.

Baines headed toward the open doorway. He was nearly there when Elena spoke again.

"Carter."

The man's step faltered for the slightest of moments.

"You never did say what it was you left here."

"It doesn't matter," Baines shot back over his shoulder.

"It must've if you came all the way out here to get it."

"It doesn't matter anymore."

"Well, if I find anything I'll be sure to pass it on," Elena said with sugary sweetness.

Baines didn't acknowledge the comment. Stomping over the threshold, he disappeared into the midday sun.

Matt and Elena both remained where they were in the wake of the man's departure. Finally, the sound of a vehicle door slamming, followed by an engine starting, reached them.

Matt watched Elena relax slightly. "You okay?"

Elena waved a hand. "I'm fine."

Matt couldn't help but be impressed she'd remembered that detail in the heat of the man's comments. He had forgotten about it himself.

"Do you really think he left anything here?"

"I'm not sure. I haven't had time to go through the place and clean up since everyone cleared out, something I should have mentioned earlier," she said with a trace of apology.

"It was fine," he told her. "I've certainly slept in worse places."

"So there could be something here. But if he didn't leave anything, then that just means he came out here to cause trouble."

"Did you have problems with him before?"

"I was never his favorite person. He was tight with Bobby, so I'm sure he was treated to plenty of complaining about me."

"He said as much," Matt confirmed. "Nice guy you married. It seems he made you the fall guy for all the money problems the ranch was having."

Her mouth tightened into a thin line. "Things were tense between us the past several years."

He nearly snorted. "I guess so."

"He wasn't always like that," Elena said quickly, lowering her eyes, her expression softening.

Matt couldn't believe she was defending the guy. Anger churned in his gut. "I hope not," he said sharply. "He had to have treated you a lot better at the beginning if you were willing to marry the guy after three months. I know for a fact you wouldn't do that with just anybody."

As soon as the words came out he would have given

anything to take them back. He hated how petty they were, how childish. He hated how jealous he sounded, and that even he could hear the thread of pain in his voice. And most of all, he hated that wounded look that entered her eyes, and knowing that he'd managed to hurt her.

"You were never 'just anybody'," she whispered.

"Just not good enough," he said before he could stop himself.

"That's not true."

Her denial only stoked the fire he was trying to tamp down, the need to know. "Really? I must have been lacking something Weston had. Was it just the money?"

"No. I didn't marry Bobby because of money."

"Then why did you do it?"

"It's…complicated—"

"How complicated can it be? What was so damn great about him that you were willing to marry him after three months—"

"He was the first man who made me feel anything after—"

She slammed her lips together, her eyes flying to his face.

He stared back, a sick feeling in his gut.

She didn't have to finish. He knew what she'd been about to say.

The implications of it hit him hard, throwing everything he'd assumed about her into a new light. Even more than before, he wished he hadn't asked, wished he'd just let it be. Felt like hell for having forced her to admit something she clearly hadn't wanted to as she stood there, the blood drained from her face.

Oh, hell. He didn't know what to say. He didn't know

if he should try to apologize, if there was some way he could make it better, even while he was still trying to process what it all meant.

From the looks of her, it looked like he'd said more than enough already.

He needed to get out of here. He needed to think.

She lowered her head again, turning her face away. It didn't look like she wanted to deal with him, either.

Matt cleared his throat. "I should make a run into town. I figured I'd pick up some paint and take care that mess on the front of your house."

"Sounds like a good idea," she murmured.

Grabbing his keys, he nodded tersely, moved for the door and escaped into the sunlight beyond.

As she had when Carter left, Elena stayed where she was. But this time it wasn't caution that held her in place. It was sheer humiliation.

She couldn't have moved if she tried, every muscle in her body tightened hard with it. She stood motionlessly and listened as Matt got into his truck and drove away. She suspected there was some paint somewhere around the ranch they could use, but she didn't bother mentioning it. She knew it was just an excuse to get out of here—away from her—for a while. At the moment she could use the time apart from him as much as he could.

Even when the sounds of the truck receded and it was clear he was gone, she remained locked in place.

She couldn't believe she'd admitted that. She'd tried not to, but he'd kept pushing and pushing, until it had just come out. Almost subconsciously she'd managed to cut off the words at the last possible moment, instinct closing up her throat, though it was still too damnably late. She hadn't had to. From the expression on his face, he knew what she'd been about to say as well as she did.

He was the first man who made me feel anything after you.

It was utterly, painfully true, a truth she would give anything for him not to know. Because it spoke volumes about just how much he'd meant to her, just how hurt she'd been after he'd gone, and she wanted to hold on to what little pride she had left too much to admit it.

Because she *had* hurt. In the months after he left, after she went back to school and tried to resume her life, she'd hurt more than she could have possibly imagined. She'd felt gutted, as though all of her insides had been torn out, and most days she barely felt capable of standing. She'd cried, racking sobs that seemed to be ripping out what was left of her, more than she had when her mother had left. Time had passed, and there were days when she'd thought she was finally getting over it—over him. Then the shooting pain in her chest, the gaping emptiness, and the tears would return. For almost a year, she'd gone through the motions of her life in a daze, and her best days were the ones when she was simply, blessedly numb.

And then she'd met Bobby.

He'd been undeniably good-looking, and if her reaction hadn't been anywhere near as strong as what she'd felt the first time she saw Matt, she'd definitely felt a spark. Frankly, it had been a relief, because, yes, it was the first time in nearly a year that a man had affected her in any way. She'd clung to that feeling, so glad to be feeling anything at all. Bobby had been the opposite of Matt in many ways, outgoing and happy, and it had been nice to be around someone who didn't remind her of him at all. It was only later that he'd changed. He'd been good to her, they'd had so much in common, and everything had seemed so easy between them. And when he'd asked her to marry him, she'd set aside her misgivings, telling herself she wasn't going to make the same mistake twice and let the man she loved get away.

Later, she'd come to the painful realization that it wasn't so much that she'd loved him, it was that she'd *wanted* to love him, wanted to love someone so she wouldn't hurt so much anymore because of Matt Alvarez.

God, she'd been so young. And stupid. Stupid most of all.

She'd made foolish decisions for all the wrong reasons, and caused them both so much unhappiness.

And all these years later, she was still here, still in this town, still paying for those mistakes the way she was afraid she would be the rest of her life.

Chapter Nine

Contrary to what he'd told Elena, Matt didn't head into town, deliberately turning in the opposite direction once he left the ranch. He wasn't ready to deal with the townspeople and their suspicions. More than anything he needed to get away from all of this mess for a while.

Especially Elena.

Elena.

The memory of the way she'd looked when he'd pushed her to confess, when she'd finally blurted it out, loomed in his mind, haunting him.

He was the first man who made me feel anything after...

After Matt. It was the only possible answer, the only thing that would have gotten that reaction from her, caused the look of horror at having spoken it. Letting him know that losing him had hurt her so much she hadn't felt anything for a year, that she'd married a man simply because he'd made her feel something, anything, again after Matt had walked away from her.

He'd hurt her that much. Just as he'd hurt her today.

The sad thing was, at one point he would have believed he wanted to hurt her, just as much as she'd hurt him. But knowing that he had, not even realizing he had or how much, he would give anything to take it back.

What's more, everything he'd assumed about her relationship with Weston had been wrong. He'd figured either she truly had loved Weston or it really had been for the money, seemingly the only possible explanations. Either way, he'd just wanted her to admit it, needed her to say in plain words the reason she'd chosen another man when she hadn't chosen him.

She finally had. But even with the possibilities he'd considered, he hadn't expected the answer.

He should have known better. He should have known her.

Matt kept driving aimlessly, trying to sort through his thoughts, trying to work out his mixed emotions. He passed by the Nolan spread where he'd worked the summer he'd met Elena. She'd said they weren't there anymore. He half wondered where they might have gone and who owned the place now. Not that he really cared or that it mattered.

It was the name of the next ranch he passed that truly caught his interest, providing a welcome distraction from what had happened with Elena.

Marshall Ranch.

The only Marshall he'd heard of in the area was Glen, the man he'd met at Elena's yesterday. The man whose eagerness to buy the ranch out from under her still struck him as suspicious.

Matt considered where he was, gauging his distance from her ranch. Yes, it was far enough from her property to be the one she'd described, and sure enough, it seemed unlikely Marshall could want a spread so far from his own for any reasons but the one she'd given.

But at the moment, Matt wasn't inclined to believe anyone would be willing to pay a sizeable amount for a ranch simply out of the goodness of his heart.

He'd figured he'd like to talk to Marshall at some point, try to suss out the man's actual motives. As long as he was out here, this seemed as good a time as any. And now that he knew Carter Baines was working out here, he couldn't help wonder if Marshall had something to do with the man's unexpected appearance that morning.

Making the turn, he thought about how he was going to approach this. By the time he pulled up in front of the house, he had a workable plan.

He was in luck. Marshall came striding out of the barn just as Matt put the truck in Park. Whether it was because his arrival had already been noticed or the man just happened to be coming out at that particular moment, Matt didn't know. Either way, Marshall looked up and spotted him as Matt stepped out of the truck. Marshall headed toward him, his movements unhurried and relaxed.

"Mr. Alvarez," Marshall called out. Somehow, Matt wasn't surprised the man had remembered his name. "What brings you here?"

"We had some trouble out at Elena's place last night and I was hoping to get your help."

Matt didn't miss the way the man's mouth tightened slightly when he referred to the ranch as "Elena's place." Apparently, Elena should consider herself part of the Weston family, but the ranch was in no way hers as far as Marshall was concerned. Matt had to wonder whether he truly thought of her as a Weston, or if it had been a line he'd been feeding her to butter her up.

"Why don't you come in?" the man said. He nodded toward the house, then turned and led the way, leaving Matt to follow.

Once inside, Marshall led Matt down a hallway to the rear of the house, opening a door on what was obviously his study. It was a comfortable, masculine space, with a fireplace, dark wood paneling and brown leather chairs. A big desk sat along the far edge of the room.

Marshall motioned for Matt to enter first, then followed him in, closing the door behind them. "Now then," Marshall said, turning to face him. "What is it you think I can help you with?"

"Like I said, we had some trouble last night. Vandalism. Somebody painted the word *Murderer* on the front of her house."

Marshall swore lightly under his breath. "This town just won't give her a break, will it?"

"But you will?"

"I beg your pardon?"

"Elena said you made an offer on the ranch, said you'd advance some of the money from the sale for her so she could use it for her defense if she needs it. That's a very generous offer."

"It's the right thing to do," he said modestly.

"So you don't believe Elena killed her husband?"

The man hesitated for a split second—long enough for Matt to notice—before shaking his head with a sound of exasperation. "No, not at all. She wouldn't have it in her."

"Sounds like you're the only person around here who believes that."

"Yes, well, the Westons are—" he cringed "—*were* highly regarded around here, and Elena's folks weren't.

Unfortunately, most people are inclined to expect the worst of her. Plus most of them just want somebody to be held responsible for Bobby's murder, and she's the most obvious person to have done it."

"But not you?

"I'd rather have the right person charged than just anybody."

Marshall was saying all the right things and sounded genuine enough, but Matt couldn't decide if he believed him. He wondered if his inclination to be suspicious was getting the best of him, leading him to read things into nothing.

But then there was Carter Baines's presence at Elena's place. Why had he really been there, and had Marshall known about it?

"Elena said you were close with the Westons."

"I knew Bobby all his life, and his brother, Jim Junior, too. Their daddy, Big Jim, was like a brother to me."

"And that's why you want the land?"

Marshall nodded. "I'd hate to see it sold off and broken up, which is what might happen if the bank takes it. That was a real possibility for Bobby, though he'd never admit it, and it won't be any easier for Elena."

"I'm sure Big Jim would have appreciated the gesture."

Marshall smiled faintly. "I doubt it. Jim always intended the land to stay in the family. Talked about how it'd always been owned by Westons and always would be." He shook his head sadly. "Of course he had no way of knowing how things would turn out for him and his boys. The past twenty years it's been one bad thing after another. It's almost like they're cursed or something."

"What do you mean?"

With a sigh, Marshall turned and moved over to a wall covered with framed photographs. He stopped in front of one of them, staring at it hard. "I don't know how much you know about the family. First Jim died so young. Heart attack at forty-two. Then his older boy, Junior, got sick. Now Bobby getting killed. Twenty years ago there was every reason to believe the Westons would be around for generations. Now they're all gone."

Marshall's voice was heavy with pain. Wanting to see what he was looking at, Matt came and stood beside him. The photo showed a group of people, a few parents and several children, at what looked like a picnic, posing for the camera. The two men were younger versions of Marshall and Big Jim, whom he recognized from pictures he'd seen on the walls of the Weston house. Based on the pose, the women were their wives, with their respective children all around them, as if they were all part of one family. Elena had said Marshall was close to the Westons and cared deeply about the family. That seemed apparent enough from the fact that he'd kept this photo, hung it on his wall.

Matt raised his eyes to scan the other pictures. Most featured children he assumed were Marshall's at various ages. One photo in particular caught his eye. Three men with their arms slung around each other, grinning at the camera. To the left was Marshall, with Big Jim in the middle. And on the right—

"Is that the sheriff?" Matt asked, pointing toward the third man in the photograph.

Marshall looked where he indicated. "Yep, that's

Walt. Of course, he wasn't the sheriff back then. He was fresh with the department. But that's him."

"So Big Jim was friends with Walt, too."

"Oh, yeah. Jim and Walt went way back. Used to go on hunting trips, fishing trips together every few months."

"You didn't go with them?"

Marshall grinned. "My wife didn't look too kindly on the idea of me taking off and leaving her with five kids to handle so I could go out and shoot things. Jim's wife passed when Bobby was still young, but he had a housekeeper who could watch over the boys for a few days, and Walt never married. It was easier for them."

Matt nodded, staring hard at the image of Walt with his arm around Big Jim's shoulder, a big grin on his face. This was the man in charge of Elena's fate, Big Jim's old hunting buddy. So Travis wasn't the only one who might have a personal stake in the case. He wondered why she hadn't mentioned it. Then again, given how long Big Jim had been dead, it was possible she didn't know. She would have been just a girl back then. Or maybe she just didn't consider it a strong enough motive for the sheriff to be taking the case personally.

Which he probably was. Great. Something else standing in the way of Elena getting a fair shake around here. No wonder they were gunning for her so hard. They were all letting their personal feelings get in the way of conducting an honest investigation.

The picture was a potent reminder of just how badly he needed to get to the bottom of this before Walt could railroad her into jail.

"By the way," he said, changing the subject. "Did you hire a man named Carter Baines?"

Marshall nodded. "Sure. I knew he'd worked for Bobby for years, and after Elena couldn't afford to keep him on anymore, he came looking for a job so I hired him. What about it?"

Another good deed for the Westons and their friends? Matt couldn't help thinking. "He showed up unexpectedly at Elena's place this morning, popped up in the bunkhouse claiming he left something there and wanted to go through the place. And when Elena noticed he was there and turned up, he insulted her."

Marshall grimaced. "I'll talk to him, make it clear I don't want anyone working for me to go bothering people like that."

"I appreciate it. Actually, he seemed to really dislike her. I was wondering if he was the type to go running around vandalizing somebody's house?"

"Carter? Nah," Marshall scoffed. "He's not the kind to go sneaking around pulling stuff like that. If he doesn't like somebody, he'll tell them to their face, as you unfortunately saw today."

Having seen the man's behavior toward Elena today, Matt could see Marshall had a point. Still, he wasn't quite willing to dismiss the possibility that a man with a nasty streak like Baines had shown would be above some dirty tricks.

"Well, you know this town better than I do. Any ideas who might be angry enough to have done that to her?"

Marshall sent him a wry look. "Pick up a telephone book."

"It's that bad?" Matt said, saying it as a question even though the man was only confirming what he already suspected.

"People are upset. Upset that nobody's been arrested, upset that she's still running around free. And they're only getting madder. I've never seen things this bad around here. I'm afraid until an arrest is made, things are only going to get a lot worse before they get better."

"You mean until *Elena* is arrested?"

Marshall gave a light shrug, his expression slightly regretful. "Somebody. I don't know if it has to be her, but somebody has to pay."

THIS TIME WHEN ELENA HEARD THE sound of an engine approaching the house, she felt no anticipation, only the familiar dread. Matt had been gone only an hour, and she wasn't expecting him back so soon. If it was him, she wasn't quite ready to face him, not sure what she was going to say.

As soon as she saw who it was, every thought of her conversation with Matt faded away, overshadowed by what faced her in the immediate future.

It was the sheriff's car. As it came closer she could make out two figures in the front seat.

Walt and Travis. Here for their daily visit.

Heck, this really should be routine to her by now, she acknowledged fatalistically. But every time she saw them coming, she knew the visit would be no more pleasant than their last and wondered what fresh surprises they might have to spring on her. Or if this would be it, the time they came to make an arrest.

She studied them carefully as they disembarked from the car, trying to prepare herself for what was to come. What she saw did nothing to ease her mind. Walt wasn't quite smiling, but he seemed happy somehow in a way that made her distinctly uneasy.

Travis, on the other hand, didn't seem happy at all. She hadn't thought it possible for him to look at her with any more hatred than he'd been treating her to the past few weeks, but somehow he was managing it, his face red, his eyes burning with rage.

"Afternoon, Elena," Walt said with false politeness.

"Sheriff. Travis," she acknowledged, nodding to them each in turn.

Travis didn't say a word in response, simply glaring at her with such undisguised fury her stomach sank even further.

Unlike his deputy's unwavering focus, Walt made a show of glancing around the area. "Your new hand around? What's his name again? Alvarez?"

Elena didn't doubt for a second that he knew exactly what Matt's name was. Not about to admit they had her on edge, she tried to keep her voice as even as possible and replied, "Yes, Alvarez. And no, he's not here. He went into town for some paint. As you can see, we have some damage to repair around here." She gestured toward the wall beside her.

Both men's eyes flicked briefly to the wall, though they must have seen what was there when they pulled up. If they hadn't already known. Travis's mouth curved in a cruel smile, so much that she almost expected him to release a bark of laughter. Walt betrayed no reaction, his eyes revealing nothing as they glanced at it then returned to her.

"Looks like you had some trouble," Walt said mildly.

"That's right. Any chance you'd feel like investigating that?"

The sheriff simply shrugged. "If you didn't see who

did it, probably not much chance of figuring out who it was. Most likely just teenagers playing a prank."

"Between this and what happened to my tires in town, the teenagers around here sure are busy," she said drily. "I wonder what they're going to have to pull before you do something about it."

"If you don't feel safe around here anymore, I'm sure you'll feel a lot safer in jail," Travis said. "All you have to do is tell us the truth about Bobby."

Elena stared back at him. "I have told you the truth about Bobby."

Travis's face reddened further, his hands fisting at his sides. He took a step toward her. "You lying b—"

"Travis," Walt cut him off without raising his voice. Travis seemed to regain control with visible effort, clamping his mouth shut and falling back into line at Walt's side. His eyes, narrowed to slits, never moved from Elena's face, his own remaining red.

"It's a shame your hand isn't here," Walt continued calmly, his tone instantly making her wary. She almost would have preferred Travis's open aggression to Walt's lightly insinuating caginess. "You never did say how you met him."

"He showed up when I needed him," Elena said easily.

"Right after your husband was murdered."

"Not quite," she returned. "It was almost two weeks later."

"And how did he just happen to show up right now, when you *needed* him?"

And just like that, she knew. He knew who Matt was, about their prior relationship. The trap Walt was laying for her was too obvious, Travis's eagerness—the way he was practically salivating at the idea of catching her in a lie—too clear. She suddenly understood his fresh anger all too well, as a chill rolled through her, her belly tightening with fear. It was exactly as she'd worried about. They knew about her and Matt—and it looked just as bad as she'd known it would.

It would look even worse if she lied about it, as they plainly expected her to. Her only hope was to go on the offensive. "Someone sent him a newspaper story about Bobby's death."

"And why would he care about Bobby's *murder?*" Walt asked, clearly making the distinction.

"Because we knew each other eight years ago. He was here in Western Bluff back then, working a summer for the Nolans. We dated that summer."

Neither Walt nor Travis had an immediate response to that, and she saw that she'd caught them off-guard. A small sense of satisfaction pushed away some of the fear.

Travis soon regained himself, his expression hardening back into a sneer. "So your old boyfriend just happens to show up right after your husband's murdered? You expect us to believe that's a coincidence?"

"No, I don't. I don't believe it's a coincidence at all. Someone sent him a newspaper story about Bobby's death to get him to come here."

Travis all but laughed. "Yeah, you!"

"It wasn't me. I hadn't had any contact with him in eight years. I had no idea where he even was."

"But somebody else just happened to and decided he should know?"

"Evidently."

"The man hasn't been in contact with you for eight years, and one newspaper article is all it takes to get him to run back to town?"

There was only one answer she could give to that. "Yes," she said simply.

This time he did laugh, the sound full of rage and no humor whatsoever. "You have to think we're idiots!"

Yes, she thought, though she wasn't about to say it out loud. "It's what happened."

"So an old boyfriend gets a story telling him your husband is dead and he hightails it to your side? Now why would he do that if you haven't seen each other or been in touch for years?"

"Because he knew I was no killer. He knew me for only three months and he knew that much. You both have known me a lot longer, so you should know it, too, even better than he does!"

"Yeah, well, we don't *know* you the same way he does," Travis sneered, the word filled with every drop of innuendo possible. "But rest assured, I do know you. I've known exactly what you were since the moment you hooked up with Bobby. I knew you were nothing but a no-good, worthless—"

"That's enough, Travis," Walt said, though there was no censure in his tone. "Now, Elena, you have to admit this story is hard to believe."

"It's the truth."

"Uh-huh," he drawled slowly. "And I suppose Alvarez can produce this mysterious newspaper article he received."

"Yes," she said. "I saw the envelope myself, complete with Western Bluff postmark."

"I look forward to seeing that," Walt said. "Why didn't you tell us any of this yesterday? You had to know it wouldn't look good when I figured it out."

"That's exactly why I didn't say anything. I didn't want you to jump to the wrong conclusions. How *did* you figure it out?"

"I'll admit it took me a while. Then I remembered that fella you were seeing that your daddy got riled up about and it all came back to me."

Exactly as Matt had suggested, she thought.

Walt eyed her shrewdly. "Pretty amazing that this guy would come back eight years later after all that trouble if he hadn't been in touch with you, just because somebody sent him a newspaper article."

Elena couldn't argue with that. "So it is."

"Indeed. When do you expect Alvarez back?"

"He didn't say."

"I guess we'll come back later then."

"Maybe we'll run into him in town," Travis said, the words sounding every bit like a threat.

"Maybe," Elena said mildly.

"Oh, and Elena?" Walt turned back with a casualness she didn't buy for a moment. "In case you or your new hand start to get any ideas about leaving town, don't."

"I'm not going anywhere." It seemed strange to say it, as long as she'd wanted out of this town. But even if she had the ability to leave, even if all her meager resources weren't connected to the ranch, she wasn't leaving now. Because she wasn't guilty, and damned if she'd convince anyone in this town that she was by running.

The look he shot her said he didn't believe her. She

wasn't surprised, nor did she bother to waste her breath arguing. She'd let her actions speak for themselves.

She wasn't her mother. She wasn't running. Not from this.

Not from anything.

Chapter Ten

When Matt finally made it into town, he took his time at the hardware store, ignoring the stares of the cashier and some of the other customers. Finding the right color of paint to match the front of Elena's house wasn't an easy task since he was operating from memory and so many of the shades were only slightly different from one another, but he wanted to get it right. He figured he could do that much for her.

He was finally loading up his truck, putting the cans of paint he'd bought in the truckbed, when he heard voices, the sounds of two men in conversation approaching on the sidewalk behind him. He didn't pay much attention to them and was about to close the tailgate when he heard one of them mention the sheriff.

"I'm telling you, Henry, you need to put more pressure on Walt and get him to make a damn arrest already. That woman should be locked up."

Matt froze, instantly tuning in to what they were saying. There wasn't a doubt in Matt's mind what woman the man was referring to.

Figuring it would look suspicious if he was just standing there not doing anything, he started acting like he was moving things around in the back of the truck without making any noise, keeping his ears peeled the whole time.

"Come on, Jack," the second man said. "Walt is doing his best. He wants her behind bars as much as we all do. He just has to get all the evidence together. You should understand that. You're a lawyer."

A lawyer named Jack. That sounded familiar. Matt quickly made the connection in his head. Elena had mentioned the lawyer in charge of Weston's will, the only lawyer in town. His name was Jack. Jack Landry. Weston's cousin.

"I understand it shouldn't be taking this long," Landry insisted. "It's been two weeks! Damn it, Henry. There has to be something you can do."

The man he called Henry sighed. "I'm just the mayor of this town, Jack. I can't force Walt to make an arrest before he's good and ready."

"Still, you—"

The other man cut him off, suddenly raising his voice, calling out. "There you are, hon. I was just on my way to meet you."

Curious, Matt gave a casual glance over to see who he was speaking to.

A woman was slowly making her way down the sidewalk toward them. It was the woman he'd spotted yesterday, the one who'd been looking at him.

Which was exactly what she was doing now.

Their eyes locked for a few seconds before she looked away, working up a smile as she turned her attention to the men as they met each other.

"Hi there," she said, kissing one of the men on the cheek—Henry, Matt figured—then nodding to the other. "Hello, Jack."

"Lynda," he acknowledged, barely concealing his annoyance that his conversation with the other man had been interrupted.

Matt studied the lawyer closely. He was roughly in his forties, with dark brown hair thinning on top. His desire to see Elena arrested for his cousin's murder made sense, but Matt couldn't help but look askance at anyone who was working against her, wondering if there wasn't more to his actions than it seemed.

Lynda turned back to Henry, who Matt assumed was her husband based on their interactions. "Ready for lunch?"

"I sure am." He gave a perfunctory glance at the other man. "I'll see you, Jack."

"Henry," Jack acknowledged.

The mayor and his wife started to turn away. Just before they headed down the sidewalk, she glanced at Matt one more time, this time quickly looking away.

He watched her go for a few seconds. Lynda, the mayor's wife. He'd have to ask Elena about her. She had to know who the woman was, might know if there was any particular reason for her attention.

Elena. He swallowed a sigh, reminded again how they'd left things, the mess he had to clean up. If they were going to talk about anything, that was probably going to be it. And he still didn't know what to say.

Even so, it was high time he got back. He finally closed the tailgate and turned away from the back of the truck.

When he arrived back at the ranch, Elena was walking across the yard heading toward the house, a bucket filled with what looked like cleaning supplies in one hand. She looked up at his approach, stopping in front of the steps to the house and waiting for him to get out of the truck.

Matt tried to gauge her expression, but couldn't read a thing from it. She was too contained, her face blank. Steeling himself, he climbed out of the truck.

"I cleaned out the bunkhouse," she said as he walked up, lifting her pail. "It should be a little more suited for occupation now."

"Thanks."

"Found this lodged between one of the dressers and a wall." She held up an item in her left hand. It was a belt buckle. "I think I've seen Carter wearing it before. I'm guessing this is what he came to get."

"So he really was looking for something he left behind," Matt said. It clearly wasn't just a belt buckle, but one he'd won at some point. Matt could understand why he'd come looking for it, even if he wasn't quite ready to assume there was no other reason the man had come poking around.

"Evidently. I'll send it on to Glen's so he gets it and won't have any other reasons to drop by." She didn't say anything for a few seconds, dropping her head and taking a deep breath. For a moment, Matt was sure he knew what she was about to say. She was going to bring up what had happened before.

She looked up and met his eyes. "Walt and Travis were here."

It wasn't what he'd expected her to say, and he couldn't hide his surprise, both at what she hadn't said and what she had. Then the implications of her words sank in, anger that he hadn't been here replacing his surprise. He knew whatever happened, it couldn't have been pleasant for her. Her expression confirmed that much. "What happened?"

"They know about you…about our history together. Just as I thought, it made things look even worse. Now they're even more convinced I killed Bobby."

"How'd they find out?"

"Walt said he remembered the fuss my father caused over our relationship back then. When he started looking into your background, it all came back to him."

"Or it never left," Matt said slowly.

Her frown deepened. "What do you mean?"

"Who better to track me down than a sheriff with police resources?"

"You think Walt's the one who sent you that article and brought you here?"

"Could be. It would explain how the person who sent the article knew where to find me. If he had something to do with Bobby's death and wanted to make you look bad, getting me to come here probably was a good way to do it."

"But Walt still doesn't have any kind of motive as far as I can tell. And why would he even bother to go to all that trouble when he'd already have plenty to try to frame me with here, especially since he had no reason to believe you would come?"

"I don't know," Matt admitted. "It's just a thought."

"I'm sure you're right about one thing, though. I knew whoever brought you here wasn't doing it to help me."

"Are you sorry I'm here?" he asked gently. He wouldn't blame her if she was. Not with the trouble his presence meant for her. Not after what had happened that morning.

Her eyes flickered to his face, then held, stroking over his skin intensely. He went still inside, not sure he wanted to know the answer.

No, that was a lie, he acknowledged. He knew what he wanted the answer to be. He just couldn't bring himself to admit it.

"No," she said finally. "No, I'm not."

The tightness that had gathered in his chest eased. "Good," he said. "Because somebody might not have intended for my presence to help you, but that's exactly what I'm going to do."

"What do you want to do?"

"Same thing as before. Get to the bottom of this. If the sheriff is even more determined to pin this on you, then we just have a little more motivation to solve this thing quicker."

Her lips twitched humorlessly. "I didn't really need any more motivation, but all right."

Matt suddenly recalled the conversation he'd overheard in town, the reminder that it wasn't just the sheriff who was out to put this on her. It was seemingly everybody in town, which she already knew. They might not need any more motivation, but they certainly had plenty of it.

Unfortunately, they were out of leads at the moment. He wasn't sure where they could go from here.

Then he looked up and saw the now-familiar word still screaming from the front of the house in bloodred paint.

MURDERER.

No, they didn't need more motivation. The crude vandalism was evidence of that. But at least that was something they could do.

He nodded at the wall. "I should take care of that. I got the paint. I'll get started now."

She followed his gaze. "Good idea. I'll help you. It'll be faster that way, and I want it gone as soon as possible. Just let me just put this inside," she said, indicating the bucket. "I'll be right back."

He watched her go, unable to help admiring her walk, glad to see the confidence, the purpose, back in her stride as she quickly climbed the front steps and moved into the house.

The fact that she looked damn good in a pair of jeans didn't hurt, either.

He shook his head, quickly turning away to start unloading the paint from the truck. Those were exactly the kind of thoughts he couldn't be having, for both their sakes. Things were messy enough between them.

He hadn't apologized for earlier, he realized, hadn't made it up to her. They seemed to have moved past it, and he doubted she'd be interested in bringing up what had happened any more than he really did. It didn't matter. That look on her face remained with him, reminding him just how carefully he had to tread from now on. He had no interest in seeing that look on her face again.

He'd hurt her enough. He wasn't going to do it again.

Chapter Eleven

A little after one-thirty in the morning, Matt made another slow circle around the house. He'd started his
watch early that night, earlier than what he suspected
was necessary, but he wasn't taking any chances. The
night before, the vandal had shown up after two. If he
made a return appearance tonight, it would likely be
around the same time or later, deeper into the night,
but it could be earlier, too. Either way, Matt wanted to
be ready.

He doubted he'd be getting much sleep tonight anyway. After everything that had happened that day, there
was too much going on in his head, too much on his
mind. Weston. Marshall.

Elena.

Stopping in front of the house, Matt breathed deeply,
pulling the air into his lungs to clear his thoughts, and
stared out over the yard. As he stood there, a vague
sense of unease washed over him, making his skin
crawl in response.

He didn't have to wonder about its cause, as he took
in the shadows surrounding him, the dark spaces nearby
untouched by lights or the moon where anyone could
be lurking, hiding. He didn't sense anyone watching,

but his skin still tingled with awareness, the feeling of danger heavy in the air, the knowledge that trouble could be moments away.

Turning slightly, he glanced back at the house. They'd managed to get the front repainted. It seemed the fastest and easiest way to cover the graffiti, which was what mattered most. The paint he'd found almost matched the wall's original color. He doubted Elena would forget the message had been there, but she had seemed relieved not to have to look at it anymore.

They'd worked well together, he thought, his mouth curving at the memory. First painting the wall, then taking care of things around the ranch. They'd fallen into a natural rhythm that had come easily, picking up each other's cues, working in sync. It had been nice. He probably shouldn't think about it, give it more meaning than it deserved, but he couldn't deny it was true.

The lights were on in the house. He was sure she was still up, probably keeping a watch of her own. Maybe even looking back at him…

With a sigh, he turned away. He needed to keep moving. Not only was there plenty of ground he needed to cover, but it was the only hope he'd have of occupying his mind and thinking of anything else.

Distracted, he heard the muffled footsteps a split second too late.

It was the flash of motion that caught his eye, the sense that something was coming at him—fast.

He started to turn, spotting something arcing toward his head—

He automatically lifted his right arm to block the blow. Instead of his head, the object—hard, metal—slammed into his forearm. Pain exploded in the bone and shot up to the shoulder, his whole body seeming to be jarred by the hit. He reeled back on his heels, a reflexive roar of agony rising into his throat.

There was no time to release it or reach for the gun in his waistband. The attacker was already coming at him again, raising his arm to land another blow.

Seeing it coming, Matt erupted into motion. He threw out his left arm, aiming for the arm wielding the object, blocking it before the attacker could bring it down. Almost at the same time, he pivoted, sending his right elbow straight into the intruder's gut. The bastard folded over with a grunt. Before he could straighten, Matt brought his left arm down, the force of the hit making the guy lose his grip on the object in his hand.

With a growl of rage, the intruder lunged forward, his head still bent, driving his fist in Matt's ribs. Stomach tensing against the pain, Matt quickly returned the blow, then another, and another as the man came back throwing punches. They circled round each other, arms thrashing, hands landing punches and grabbing at clothes.

He caught only flashes of his opponent as they grappled. Tall. Broad shoulders. Black clothes. Ski mask covering the face. No way to identify him. More than anything he wanted to rip off the mask, see the bastard's face. The drive fueled him with every punch he threw, each one he dodged. He didn't care about getting hurt. Fending off blows was all about being able to get to the guy. Matt had to get to him, had to take him down. He had to be stopped.

"Hey!"

The woman's voice came as if from a great distance. He barely heard it over the thumping of his heartbeat as he battled with the intruder, unable to slow for an instant, not willing to give an inch.

In the far recesses of his mind, the identification was made.

Elena. She was out here.

The thought only pushed him to fight harder. She shouldn't be here. It was dangerous. This bastard was dangerous. He wanted to hurt her—

A gunshot sliced through the air, the noise nearly deafening.

Matt and his opponent froze simultaneously, both shocked into stillness by the loudness, the nearness of the gunshot.

What had happened? Had someone been shot—

The intruder recovered first, landing a blow to Matt's gut, which he never saw coming. Pain ripped through his abdomen, his body automatically folding over in response. The bastard gave him a hard shove, sending him crashing to the dirt.

Matt had barely landed before he was putting his hands out to ground himself, shoving the pain aside, ready to push back to his feet. Raw fury pulsing through him, he jerked his head up, already searching for his opponent, prepared to launch himself back into the fray—

Only to see the intruder making a break for it, sprinting toward the barn.

"Stop!" the female voice shouted.

The intruder didn't obey, vanishing into the shadows on the side of the barn.

Matt swallowed the curse he really wanted to yell at the top of his lungs. Not only had the bastard gotten the better of him—and that was reason enough for his fury—but he'd gotten away, free to come back and try something again.

Seconds later, he heard Elena hurry over, sensed her crouching at his side.

"Matt? Are you okay?"

He turned to look at her. She sat on her haunches, her gun still clutched in her right hand. With the moon shining down over her shoulders, she looked like some kind of avenging angel.

He sat up, grimacing as his body groaned in protest. "You shouldn't have come out here. You could have been hurt."

"Me? You were the one in a knock-down, drag-out fight." Rising to her feet, she extended her hand to him to help him up. "Come into the house. I have some pain relievers. I have a feeling you could use some."

"I'm fine," he said.

"I don't believe you."

He looked up at her. She stood there, hand extended, waiting.

Finally, with a groan, he took it. For a moment the feel of her soft hand in his threw him, and he nearly groaned again.

Soft. God, she was soft.

Then he felt her start to tug to help him to his feet. He nearly shook himself. Maybe the intruder had landed a blow to the head, knocking the sense out of him, without him noticing. He was starting to feel a little woozy.

He let her help without giving her his full weight. If he did, he'd only pull her down on top of him, and then…

No, that wouldn't be good at all.

Once he was on his feet, she released his hand all too soon and started for the house, leaving him to follow.

As he started to, Matt glanced behind him into the darkness. He wondered if the intruder was gone or lingering in the shadows, watching.

Just in case it was the latter, Matt did his best to hide how sore he felt, walking to the front steps as smoothly as possible. After he'd climbed them, he turned back, planted his legs on the porch's wooden planks, and slowly scanned the night, sending a message to the bastard.

He'd gotten away twice now.

He wasn't getting away a third.

"HAVE A SEAT," ELENA SAID, waving toward the chairs at the kitchen table. Her heart still pounding in the aftermath of what had happened, she made her way to the counter and reached in the cabinet for the bottle of pain relievers she knew was there.

Pouring a glass of water from the sink, she turned around to find Matt had done as ordered. Seeing him in the light, he didn't look as bad as she'd feared he would. His hair was a mess, his clothes rumpled, but there weren't any visible bruises or scratches on his face or neck. But then, from what she'd seen, he and his attacker had been aiming most of their blows at their torsos. As she watched him shift in his seat, wincing as he twisted his upper body, she could only imagine how bad the damage was there.

She was tempted to ask to take a look, see whether he wanted her to check his injuries. Then a shiver rolled through her at the very idea of his bare torso, and she had to admit it would be a very bad idea.

Instead, she moved to the table, placing the glass of water in front of him. She uncapped the bottle and shook out two pills, holding them out to him. From the way his lips thinned, she was convinced he was going to refuse them. Finally, with visible reluctance, he took them. She almost rolled her eyes. *Men.* Always trying to act so tough.

"Are you sure you're okay? I have a first-aid kit."

"The thing that hurts worst is my pride." He shook his head. "Can't believe he got the drop on me."

"Not really," she pointed out. "You caught him just in time to block that hit."

He raised his head. "You saw?"

She nodded, the terror of those moments coming back to her so strongly it was like she was seeing it again. She'd been at her window, unable to sleep, when she'd seen Matt walking in front of the house, then the attacker had come rushing at him from out of nowhere, the tire iron clutched in his fist, aimed at Matt's head. She'd been helpless to do anything to warn him as it had come swinging down. She didn't know how, but he'd managed to sense the attacker's ambush just in time to dodge the blow. "I wanted to say something, warn you. When I saw him coming at you with that tire iron—"

"So that's what it was," he muttered. "Hurt like hell." He automatically moved his left hand to his right arm, no doubt over the spot where the blow had landed.

"Do you want me to take a look at it?" she asked.

He shook his head. "It'll just be a bruise. I'll live."

It wasn't as though she could insist. Pulling out one of the chairs, she sank into it, facing him. "Do you figure it was the same person who spray painted that word on the house last night?"

"Most likely."

"But why? Is he just getting some kind of sick pleasure out of tormenting me?"

"It could be, especially if he really believes you killed Weston. Or maybe he doesn't intend to let you get any rest until you confess."

She exhaled sharply. "Well, that's not going to happen, so I guess I won't be getting much rest. Not that I have been anyway…" She compressed her lips together, wishing she hadn't admitted that, though she was sure he would have guessed as much. Her current circumstances didn't exactly lend themselves to a good night's sleep, even beyond the impact he was having on her dreams.

"If he comes back, I'll catch him," Matt vowed. "He's not going to get away with this."

She believed he meant it, but after witnessing that brutal fight between the two men tonight, she was more concerned about the attacker catching *Matt*. It was a miracle he wasn't hurt worse. She wasn't sure they could count on that miracle to happen again.

"He came after you, you know. If he comes back, you could be hurt further."

"I can take care of myself," he said, and again it was all she could do not to roll her eyes.

Men.

She watched him shift in his chair, wincing again, and she nearly did the same.

"Sorry," she murmured.

"Not your fault," he gritted through his teeth.

"Isn't it?" she said. "I'm sorry you got sucked into all of this—"

"I'm not," he said firmly. The vehemence in his tone made her go still. She met his eyes.

"I'm not here because somebody sent me a newspaper article or you somehow made me. I'm here because I want to be."

Her heart lodged in her throat at the intensity, the purpose, in both his response and the way he was looking at her. Staring into his eyes, the question she'd been unable to answer, the one she hadn't dared ask, popped into her mouth, and this time she couldn't stop it from coming out.

"Why?"

The single word hung there between them, heavy in the air.

He didn't answer at first, his jaw tensing, simply looking at her, his dark eyes veiled.

"I mean, after all this time, after everything that happened…"

"Because I couldn't let them do that to you," he said roughly. "I couldn't let them railroad you and send you to jail. You don't deserve that."

It was a reasonable answer. An honest answer, she was sure. But there was so much more unspoken about it, so much she could infer that she didn't know if she should, no matter how much she suddenly wanted to.

"After the way things ended, I thought you hated me," she said softly.

"I did," he admitted. "For a while. Or at least I thought I did. But that was a long time ago."

"Yes, it was." Practically a whole other life. They'd changed so much since then. Yet sometimes when she looked at him, like now, she remembered as clearly as though it had happened moments ago, and nothing had changed at all.

Or maybe that wasn't a memory, she admitted as she held his gaze, warmth flooding through her. Sometimes it seemed so vivid because it wasn't being remembered, but experienced in the present.

Matt slowly lowered his eyes, looking hard at the tabletop. "Did you ever think what would have happened if you'd come with me?"

She paused again and hesitated, uncertain how much she wanted to admit. But she couldn't lie, not to him, not at this moment. "I used to. A lot."

"And what'd you think?"

She winced. "I thought…there was no point thinking about it. I couldn't change it and do things differently, so thinking about what it would have been like wasn't going to get me anywhere."

He nodded. "That was probably smart."

"What about you?" she asked. "Did you think about what might have been?"

He didn't say anything for a long moment. "No," he said.

She certainly understood. Sometimes it was just so much easier if they didn't think about things. But she knew just as well that some things simply couldn't be forgotten.

They sat in silence for a few moments until Matt finally said, "Can I ask you something?"

"Sure."

"If things were really that bad here, why didn't you leave?"

"You mean like my mother did?" She gave her head a firm shake. "I always knew that when I got married, it was going to be forever. I wasn't going to bail if things got tough or were less than perfect. When I said those vows I meant them."

"Even if it meant being unhappy?" he asked gently.

"Even then." And there'd been the guilt, she acknowledged to herself. For having married him when she hadn't loved him as much as she should have. For making a mistake that had caused them both such unhappiness. If he'd asked for a divorce, she would have given it to him without question, without asking for anything in return. But even if she had been willing to leave, it hadn't seemed right that she be the one who made that call.

"What about him? It doesn't sound like he was any happier. Did he ever say anything about ending the marriage?"

"No. He always had enough to worry about with the ranch. I'm sure our marriage was the least of his concerns."

"Or maybe deep down he still loved you," he said quietly.

"I don't know. By the end, he sure didn't act like it." She shook her head again, not really wanting to think about Bobby for the time being. "What about you? Eight years is a long time. You must have had somebody serious in your life."

His whole body seemed to tense, then he shook his head once. "Nope."

She knew she should probably leave it alone. Of all people in the world, it was likely her business least of all. But she couldn't manage to keep from pressing, wanting to know, needing the answer. "You didn't want that?"

"Nope," he repeated.

She didn't like thinking of him alone. She wasn't naive enough to think he'd been completely without female company in those years, but there was a big difference between sex and having a meaningful relationship with someone. And he was as alone as he'd ever been.

She couldn't help but feel a pang of guilt, knowing that she must have played a part in that. Of course his childhood had left scars that had never quite healed. The difference was, despite what he'd been through, there'd still been hope for him. He'd opened up to her, opened his heart and soul to someone for the first time, trusted her.

Loved her.

And she'd thrown it back in his face.

She winced at the idea. It wasn't what she'd intended, but she'd known even back then it was how he would take it.

Maybe it was something most people would have gotten over, recovered from, over the years. But not him. Even in those early days, when they were happy from the start, he hadn't revealed his deepest self to her. It had taken months, until right before the end, before he'd let the walls down completely. It didn't surprise her he hadn't let down those walls again, had protected himself this strongly against getting hurt again. But knowing it was true didn't make her happy.

"What's your life like in New Mexico?" she asked, hoping to hear something happier.

"Good."

She almost smiled. He was still as forthcoming as ever. "So you're working on a ranch?"

He nodded. "I'm the foreman on a cattle operation

out there. A guy I worked with a few years ago hired me on when he bought his own place."

"And you're happy there?"

"Pretty much," he conceded after a while.

"But not entirely?" she asked carefully.

Again he fell quiet for a minute, this silence lasting longer than the last. "The Triple C's a good place, and Cade and Piper are good people. I know I have a place there as long as I want it. I've just been thinking lately about how long I want that to be. They just got married, and they're settling down and making all these plans. It's got me considering what I want to do. I think every man thinks about wanting something of his own someday. Maybe my own place. Maybe something else. I don't know."

It seemed some things hadn't changed, she acknowledged. His life wasn't completely settled and his future was unknown, just as it had been before. The difference was that this time his words inspired no unease in her. Maybe it was because she was different, old enough to know by now there was no certainty in this life. Maybe it was he who was different. He wasn't that young man finding his way in the world. There was something so solid about him, so strong. Everything about him spoke of a man capable of making his own way and getting things done. She had no doubt he'd decide what he wanted and get it.

Suddenly she wished she hadn't asked. Talking about the future just reminded her how uncertain her own was, and how whatever future he had wouldn't have her in it.

"I'm sure you'll figure it out," she said, pushing to

her feet. "It's getting late. We should probably try to get some sleep."

"Good idea."

Together they made their way to the front door. She was about to open it when she froze. "Do you think he'll come back? Or that he's still out there?"

"I doubt he'd come back," Matt said. "I think I got in enough solid shots that he should be nursing his wounds somewhere if he left. And he should be long gone by now."

Pulling the door open, she scanned the scene beyond, unconvinced.

An idea suddenly hit her. He should move into the house. He would be safe here. They both would be safe here, in this place where she hadn't felt truly safe from the moment she'd come home to find her husband shot dead in his study.

More important than her safety, she needed him nearby.

Needed to know he was safe.

The idea was so foolish she instantly rejected it. It would be a huge mistake. She could barely sit at the same table with him without feeling…something, something unsettling and confusing.

And exciting.

She kept her mouth shut. He moved past her and stepped outside. "Good night," he said.

"Good night," she echoed. She watched him go, tracking his progress the whole way, unable to take her eyes from the broad shoulders, the wide back and slim hips. In the yard he bent to pick up something from the ground. The tire iron, she thought with a shudder, the memory of just how close it had come to his head returning to her. So close. Too close. He turned back slightly and waved it at her, and she smiled. At least he was the one with the tire iron now. If the intruder was still around and tried coming at him, Matt would have the advantage.

She continued to watch him go until he was long out of sight, a solitary figure walking off into the moonlight, her stomach doing a little flip. And knew that everything she was feeling was new, not a memory. A response to the man he was, not the man he'd been.

The man she still ached for after all these years.

Chapter Twelve

As expected, Matt woke up sore the next morning. When he pushed himself up from the bed, his body seemed to scream in protest, every bone aching.

He swore under his breath, vowing once again that he was going to take down the intruder the next time he showed up around here.

Dressing quickly, he was just stepping out of the bunkhouse when a ringing erupted from his pocket. He fished out his phone and checked the screen.

Pam.

"Hey there."

A beat of silence echoed over the line. "You don't sound so good," she noted.

"Rough night," he muttered, starting toward the house.

"Hmm. Should I even ask how it's going, then? Any progress?"

"Not really," he said, unable to keep the frustration from his voice. "We've been asking questions, but mostly running into dead ends."

"Has your friend been arrested?"

"No." *Not yet.*

"Well, that's something at least. Things could be worse."

Matt knew she was right. He didn't even want to think about how much worse they could get. "You find anything on your end?"

"First, I got a list of highly regarded defense attorneys I can send you so you'll have them if the time comes you need them."

"Thanks," he said, inspiration striking. "I hate to ask this, but can you find the names of a few attorneys who handle estates and inheritance issues, too? We're having some issues with the lawyer in charge of Weston's estate. He's Weston's cousin and is making things difficult for Elena. I'd like to find out what her options are."

Pam was quiet for a moment. "His cousin, huh? Jack Landry? About that…"

Matt could practically hear her mind working. "What is it?"

"When his name came up as Weston's only other possible heir I thought I'd do some research into Texas state inheritance law. In Texas, being convicted of killing someone doesn't necessarily stop the killer from inheriting. But if there are other possible heirs, they can file suit and make a claim on the estate to prevent the killer from inheriting. In that case it would go to them."

Matt had no trouble following where she was going. "Which means if Elena is found guilty of killing Bobby, Landry can claim the ranch."

That certainly could explain why he was so determined to see her locked up. And if he was pushing this hard to make it possible for him to inherit, who knew what else he might have done to get the ranch.

He should have thought of it sooner. "Thanks, Pam, that's a big help."

"There's one more thing." She paused for a beat. "I also did the search you asked for on Teresa Reyes."

His pulse kicked up in anticipation. "Did you find her?"

"Nope. Not a trace in the past twenty-five years."

He didn't know which answer he'd been hoping for, but as soon as he heard Pam's answer his heart dropped. "Does that mean what I think it does?"

"Most likely," Pam said bluntly. "She's either done a perfect job covering her tracks—something I have a hard time believing she could have done without a lot of help—or she's not alive and hasn't been for the past twenty-five years."

"Do you think there could be a connection between those women who went missing back then and the disappearance of Elena's mother?"

"There could be. If there was a killer at work at the time, it's too much of a coincidence not to be considered. But then again, it was never proven that those missing women were connected or that there was a killer operating. We have to keep that in mind."

"True," he agreed. "I don't suppose there's anything more you can find out?"

"I'm already on it. I've scheduled a meeting with the agent who headed the investigation. He's retired but still in the area."

He wasn't surprised. Pam was nothing if not thorough. "Thanks, Pam. Let me know if you find anything else out?"

"Will do." As always, she ended the call without another word, their business having been concluded.

Matt took his time lowering the phone from his ear, trying to absorb this new information. If what he suspected was true, then everything Elena believed about her mother was wrong. It could change so much about how she viewed her family, her life.

"Who was that?"

He jerked his head up to find he'd reached the house without realizing it. Elena stood on the porch, arms folded over her chest. Damn. He could have used some time to process this, to think about what he would say, or if he would say anything before he knew more.

Hoping she couldn't read much in his expression, he climbed the steps to join her. "Pam Lowry. She's my boss's sister-in-law and an FBI agent who works in Dallas."

She blinked in surprise. "You know an FBI agent? Why didn't you tell me?"

"Guess it just didn't come up. I asked her to do some research for me on the town, the people…"

"And me?" she asked. There was no discernable trace of anger in her voice, only curiosity.

He nodded his confirmation. "I needed to know as much as I could about all of this as quickly as possible."

"What did she have to tell you?"

"Not much I didn't already know, unfortunately." He hesitated, not sure how to handle this, not sure whether he should tell her, not sure what it meant. "There was one thing, though…."

"What is it?" she prodded when he didn't continue.

"I asked her to look up your mother."

She simply blinked at him, her expression utterly blank. "My mother?" she repeated flatly. "Why?"

"Travis brought her up back in town on my first day

here, how she took off, so when I had somebody on the phone with the resources to track her down, I asked."

"Oh," Elena said, unable to come up with a single alternate response. She supposed she'd once wondered where her mother had gone and what she was doing, but Teresa Reyes had been gone so long now Elena seldom thought of her at all anymore. "All right then. What did your friend have to say?"

"She didn't find her," he said gently.

Elena felt no disappointment, only the same numbness that seemed to have blanketed her from the first moment he'd brought up the subject. "I guess she did a good job covering her tracks then. She really must not want to be found."

"That's just it," Matt said carefully. "She didn't just do a good job. Pam couldn't find anything at all, something that shouldn't be possible if your mother's still out there. Which means she most likely—"

"Is dead," Elena finished when he didn't. She saw the open concern in his eyes. She understood it, was even touched by it a little, even if it was unnecessary. How could she begin to mourn someone who'd been dead to her for years?

"There's more," Matt said. "Earlier I asked Pam if she could find any background information on the town, anything interesting I should know. She said there wasn't much, but Western Bluff was mentioned in connection with a number of Latino women in their late twenties to early thirties who were reported missing in the area twenty-five years ago. That's about when your mother supposedly left, isn't it?" he said when she didn't respond.

"Yes," she admitted weakly, not sure where he was going with this.

No, it was obvious where he was going with this. She just didn't like it. "What are you suggesting? That my mother didn't leave? That she was…taken?"

"I don't know. The cases were being investigated as possibly being the work of a serial killer, but no evidence was ever found of that."

"So there's a chance it might not be true."

"A chance, yes."

But not a likely one, she acknowledged. The FBI wouldn't have been looking into it if it hadn't seemed suspicious. And it would have been. This wasn't the city, there weren't all that many people in the area to begin with. For several women with at least a similar ethnic background and age to go missing in the same general area, it would seem more likely than not there was a connection.

But her mother? Was it possible she hadn't left? Had something happened…?

Elena couldn't even begin to process the significance of that. She had far too much on her mind at the moment that mattered so much more.

She did her best to push the thought aside for another time, sometime when she could try to come to terms with it. Sometime far in the future. "That's not important right now," she said. "Bobby's murder is the only thing that is."

Matt looked at her for a long moment, as though he wasn't sure about that. She steeled herself, silently willing him to let it go. She really couldn't deal with this right now. She was barely handling everything else on her plate—the ranch, Bobby's death, *him*. She couldn't cope with one more thing, especially one whose implications threatened to be this unsettling.

He finally nodded. "All right. Let's focus on the murder."

Elena exhaled, only then realizing she'd been holding her breath. "Good. Any ideas what we should do now?"

He appeared to consider the question. "About his cousin. How was Jack Landry's relationship with Bobby?"

"Decent, I suppose. They weren't close. I can't remember Jack coming out here even once since I'd been married to Bobby, but that might have had more to do with me. Jack is one of those who figured I married Bobby for his money. They got along well enough. Why you do ask?"

He quickly explained what Pam had told him about the inheritance law. She was frowning when he finished. "You think Jack might have killed Bobby to inherit the ranch?"

"It's a motive, a pretty good one. We have to consider it, especially since we don't have a lot of other leads."

"True, but the ranch isn't really worth inheriting. It's in so much debt it's not much of a prize. It's definitely not worth killing somebody over."

"From what you said and what I heard in town, I got the feeling Bobby's debts weren't exactly common knowledge. It could be Landry doesn't even know about them."

"True."

"And is it possible he knows about the offer Marshall made on the place? In that case, even if he knows about the debts, he would also know he could make money from selling it."

"It's possible. I doubt Bobby would have mentioned it, but I don't know who Glen's told."

"I want to try to talk to Landry, see if I can get anything out of him."

"Do you really think he'll talk to you?"

"I'll just have to do my best not to give him a choice. Do you want to come?"

The idea of confronting Jack the way she was feeling right now seemed like far more than she could handle at the moment. "I don't think so. Jack isn't going to talk to me. If you really think you'll get anything out of him, you're better off going on your own."

The look he gave her said he recognized it for the excuse it was. "If you're sure…"

Elena nodded. "I have enough I need to get done around here. The horses need to be fed. I need to check the stock. You know how it goes."

"Do you want me to stay…"

"No. Go. See what you can find out."

"I'll be back in a little while then."

"Okay."

He hesitated, as if there was something else he wanted to say, as if there was something he *should* say. Finally, with one final nod, he headed to his truck.

Elena watched him go. After he stepped into the vehicle, she finally released a breath she'd been holding. It didn't help. Her chest still felt tight. So very tight.

She lurched into motion, moving toward the barn. She'd meant what she'd said. She had so many things to do. And more than anything else in this world at the moment, she needed to do them.

MAYBE HE SHOULDN'T HAVE TOLD her, Matt thought as he drove away from the ranch. At least until he'd thought about what it meant and all the ramifications. He'd told himself he didn't want to hurt her, but it was obvious she'd been thrown off by the revelation at the very least. But he hadn't felt right keeping it from her.

Maybe he shouldn't have left her, but he'd had the distinct sense she wanted to be alone.

By the time he'd made it to Western Bluff, he still didn't have an answer. He finally had to set the question aside to focus on what he was going to say to Jack Landry.

Landry's law office was located on Main Street, not far from the police station. Matt remembered spotting it on his way into town. Giving the police station a wide berth, he parked at the other end of the block and made his way back to Landry's office.

Stepping inside, he found himself looking at Landry himself, recognizing him from the street the day before. The man stood at a desk in what was a small reception area, speaking to the woman seated behind it. Both of them looked up at his entrance, Landry's eyes narrowing, lips compressing into a thin, angry line. Matt supposed that meant the man knew who he was, too.

Still, he figured it would be best to go with an introduction, to try to get things off to an easy start. They were probably going to get heated soon enough.

"My name is Matt Alvarez. I'm working for Elena Weston."

"Oh, is that what people are calling it these days?" Landry snorted. "You can cut the crap, Alvarez. I know who you are."

"I'd like a word with you."

"Not interested."

"Well, I'm going to be talking. I can do it right here in front of your assistant, but I'm not sure you're going to want her to hear what I have to say, or we can do this in private."

Landry eyed him, and Matt could tell the man was gauging his seriousness, and how much he cared about whatever Matt might reveal. From the desk, the woman's head swung back and forth as she slowly looked between them.

"All right," Landry said. "I'll bite. Let's hear what you've got to say." He turned and walked through a door behind him.

Figuring that was as much of a cue to follow as he was going to get, Matt did. The second room was clearly Landry's private office. Once Matt was through the door, the lawyer closed it behind him and moved to the desk. "If you've come to declare her innocence to me, you're wasting your time—and mine."

"No, I'm here to talk about inheritances."

Stopping behind the desk, Landry glared at him. "I'm not discussing my cousin's will with you. It's privileged, not to mention none of your damn business."

"No, I want to talk about the law. See, I recently learned a little something about inheritance law here in Texas. It turns out that if a murder victim's primary heir is convicted of his murder, then another heir can petition to inherit his estate instead. Besides Elena, you're Bobby's only other living relative, aren't you?"

The man's jaw visibly tightened. "What are you suggesting?"

"Only that it gives you a motive for murder—and to see Elena put in jail for it."

The man's eyes flared in outrage. "This conversation is over."

Matt held his ground. "You were pushing pretty hard for that to happen the other day when I overheard you talking to the mayor, trying to get him to pressure the sheriff into making an arrest."

"Because she murdered my cousin. Everybody in this town knows it."

"Everybody in this town is wrong. She didn't do it."

"And we're all just supposed to take your word for it?"

"No, you can take the evidence's word. There is none."

"Yet."

"It's been two weeks and the police haven't exactly been sitting on their heels. Don't you think if there was anything to find, they would have come up with something by now?"

Landry held up a hand. "I told you you're wasting your time if you're going to argue her innocence with me. Just like you're wasting your time with the rest of that garbage you mentioned. This also is none of your business, but if it'll get you out of here, I'll go ahead and say it. What you didn't mention about that law is that the other heir has to petition to inherit, it doesn't happen automatically. I have no intention of doing that. So even when Elena is convicted—and she will be—I won't inherit, because I don't want to."

"Really?" Matt scoffed. "You expect me to believe you wouldn't take the ranch?"

"I don't care what you believe. And no, I wouldn't take the place if you paid me to."

Landry was so vehement Matt actually believed him,

the realization as surprising as the man's statement. "Why not?"

"I don't want anything from the Westons. There's too many bad vibes surrounding them. And I can't stand the ranch," Landry said frankly.

"Why?"

"I just can't. Even when I was a kid I hated going out there to visit my aunt and my cousins. There's just something about it. As long as I've been alive, nobody's been happy out there. First my aunt, Bobby's mother, was thrown from her horse and killed. She was young when she died. So were Big Jim, Junior and now Bobby. I don't know what it is. Maybe I'm just being superstitious, but the place didn't feel right to me even before my aunt died. And nothing about it has changed my mind since."

Seeing the intensity burning in the man's eyes, Matt felt a shiver roll along his skin. He didn't doubt Landry meant every word, his unease with the place communicated so loud and clear Matt could feel it himself.

He suddenly remembered the feeling he himself had had last night. He'd thought it was simply the feeling of danger, the knowledge that someone could be—and likely was—lurking in the darkness. Was it possible it was something more?

As soon as the thought occurred, he recognized how ridiculous it was. He didn't believe in curses or anything like that. Although, considering it brought back Marshall's comment yesterday. He'd said the Westons seemed like they were cursed or something. He'd been talking about the family themselves, not the ranch. Either way, Matt didn't buy it. The Westons had just had bad luck. It happened.

But looking at Landry, his face pale, his expression tense, he believed everything he was saying.

Even so, Matt hadn't come all the way here not to play all his cards. "You wouldn't have to keep the ranch. I'm sure you've heard about Glen Marshall's offer to buy it."

Landry showed no surprise. Matt took that as confirmation that Landry had already known.

"I don't want the money. Bobby was my cousin and I loved him, and he was my only living relative, too. No amount of money could make up for that. Now will that be all, or do you have any more accusations to throw at me?"

"That's it."

"The door's right there. Use it." With that, Landry finally pulled the chair out from behind his desk and sat in it, rolling forward to the desk and focusing on the papers on top of it as though Matt wasn't there.

Turning the conversation over in his mind, Matt opened the door and left. Moments later he was outside on the sidewalk.

It was possible Landry was lying, of course. He was a lawyer; chances were he was good at it. But Matt's gut told him the man had been telling the truth. Which made this just another dead end.

As he made his way back to his truck, he couldn't help but think about Landry's words. So many bad things happening to one family. Including Elena, he thought. She may not have died like the other Westons, but she'd had a rough time of it. A rough time that was still ongoing. Damn. All this, and they were still no closer to the identity of Bobby Weston's killer. And like the man had said, everybody was left still thinking Elena had done it.

He was almost at his truck when he looked up and spotted her, just as he had the last couple of days.

Lynda, the mayor's wife, the woman from the street, the woman who'd been watching him.

Just as she was now. Their eyes met once again. This time she quickly glanced away and didn't look at him again, though the deliberate way she wasn't was just as telling.

He'd asked Elena about her. She'd said the mayor's wife was a woman named Lynda Clayton and her husband's name was Henry. The two of them had never been particularly warm toward her, so Elena figured the woman's attention was no different from anyone else's, believing he was working for a murderer. Still, he couldn't escape the feeling there was more to it. Who was this woman? Why did she seem so interested in him?

With Landry's talk of curses and bad vibes ringing in his mind, he half wondered if the woman even existed, or if she was just a ghost haunting him for some reason.

No, she was definitely real, as she unlocked the Mercedes in front of her and climbed in. As he watched her start her engine, he realized that while he hadn't gotten the answer to the biggest question on his mind, he could get an answer to this one. He didn't have to ask Elena. He could go straight to the source and ask the woman herself.

She was already backing out of the space, getting ready to leave. There was only one thing he could do.

He got in his truck and followed her.

She drove to the east side of town, what he guessed was the good side judging from the look and size of the houses on the street she finally arrived on. She pulled into the driveway of one of them, and he figured that meant she was home.

He parked against the curb and quickly got out of the truck, making his way up the driveway.

She was just opening the front door when he called out, not wanting her to get inside before he could speak to her. "Excuse me, ma'am?"

She glanced up and looked back at him. He saw immediately that she recognized him, a trace of nervousness entering her eyes.

Matt smiled, trying to look reassuring. "Mrs. Clayton, is it?"

She looked at first like she wasn't sure she wanted to answer before slowly nodding. "That's right."

Something in her eyes held him. It wasn't the wariness of a woman who'd found a stranger on her doorstep. Instead, there was something speculative in her steady gaze, as though she were studying him, trying to gauge him in some way. He recognized the feeling. It was the same way she'd looked at him in town, though he was only now close enough to read it.

"Ma'am, my name is Matt Alvarez. I'm working for Elena Weston out at the Weston Ranch."

After a moment, she nodded. "Yes."

He tried to figure out what to say. "Hello, I've noticed you staring at me," wasn't really going to cut it.

Trying to find the words, he surveyed her, this attractive, well-dressed woman in her early fifties…

Which was about how old Elena's mother would be if she were still alive.

He wondered if he just had Teresa Reyes on his mind, given his conversation with Elena. But he had to admit, in a town this size, chances were the two women had known each other, maybe grown up together. He couldn't help but ask.

"By any chance did you know Elena's mother? Teresa, I believe her name was?"

The flash of emotion that passed over her face before she could hide it was all the answer he needed. Lynda Clayton not only had known Elena's mother, but the name meant enough to her to stir an emotional reaction. And suddenly he was sure he had the answer to a question he'd been asking for days.

He leaned closer, watching as her eyes widened slightly though she didn't back away, and said quietly, "You're the one who sent me the article, aren't you?"

There was no missing the flare of alarm in her gaze, but she waited too long to deny it to claim she didn't know what he was talking about. Even as she opened her mouth to respond, he spoke again.

"Do you really want to have this conversation out here? Because I'm not going anywhere. I've been wanting to talk to you from the minute I opened that envelope, and I'm not leaving until I have answers."

She didn't move, staring at him, doubt etched across her features, until he figured a softer tack might be called for. He gentled his tone.

"I believe you sent me that article because you wanted to help her. Has that changed?"

He saw immediately he'd been right. She stepped back out of the doorway, pushing the door open farther. "Come in then. Quickly."

Matt did as ordered, stepping over the threshold and

past her into the house. As soon as he had, she shut the door behind him.

"So you did send me the article," he said, still wanting the confirmation.

She nodded tersely without looking at him. "Yes. You might as well come in." She moved past him into a room on the left. It was the living room. With a heavy sense of weariness, she lowered herself into the nearest seat.

Matt remained in the entryway to the room, giving it a quick glance and checking the other entrances. There was no one in sight and a heavy silence hung over the house. Both seemed to indicate no one else was around. He doubted she would have invited him in if there was.

He refocused his attention solely on her. "Why?" he asked.

"Like you said, I wanted to help Elena."

"But why contact me?"

"Because there was no one else."

"There was you. You could have helped her."

Lynda opened her hands in a helpless gesture. "What could I do? Everyone in this town believes she killed Bobby, and no one was going to believe me just because I said otherwise. And if I started opposing Henry they'd all think I was crazy. So I did the only thing I could. I reached out to someone who might be able to do something."

"Again, why did you pick me out of all the people in the world? You could have hired her a lawyer, a private investigator…"

"I don't have the money to do either of those things. If I took the money out of our joint account, Henry would have stopped the payment, and at the very least I'd have to explain why I did it."

"Why *did* you do it? What difference was it to you?"

Lynda swallowed, her gaze becoming distant. "Teresa Reyes was my best friend growing up. I don't even know how many people remember that now, it was so long ago. When we were little girls and all through high school, she was like a sister to me. You may not know it looking at me now, but my folks were poor, and so were hers. We were two of a kind, us against all those rich, snobby mean girls. Then I started dating Henry, and things started to change. I had Henry's approval, so the rich girls started to notice me. Accept me. Teresa and I started drifting apart." She gave her head a hard shake. "No, that lets me off the hook more than I deserve. We didn't drift apart. I cut her loose. She was my best friend, and I pretty much just stopped talking to her. Our lives weren't the same anymore. We were living in different worlds, especially after she started seeing Ed, and Henry and I got married. Henry didn't want me around Teresa and especially Ed. They weren't his kind of people. The 'right' kind of people. And I went along with him. I didn't really feel like I belonged with his friends, and Teresa was kind of a reminder of why I didn't. It was easier to not be friends with her anymore. At least for me.

"Henry and I started having kids, and of course Teresa had Elena. When Teresa left Ed, ran away from her own daughter, I felt so awful. I'd seen her in town sometimes. I knew she couldn't be happy, but I had no idea things were so bad that she would decide to run away like that. She needed a friend. I should have been that friend. I should have been there for her. It was too late for that. But I could at least try to be there for Elena.

"I kept an eye on her over the years. I knew Henry wouldn't want me getting involved. That wouldn't have stopped me if I'd been able, but the one time I tried talking to Ed about her, offering to help in any way I could, he just screamed at me and threw me out of his house. He knew Teresa and I had been close, of course, and he didn't want anybody around who reminded him of her. Not to mention he remembered how I treated Teresa. He had no use for me, said I was probably one of the things in this town she'd been trying to get away from. I suppose I couldn't blame him for that at least.

"So I did what I could. Not as much as I should have, but something. Elena needed money for school, so I pulled some strings with a ladies' organization I belong to out of Dallas that offers a scholarship. It wasn't much, nowhere near as much as I would have liked. I should have tried harder. I'd hoped she'd be able to get out of Western Bluff, make a fresh start somewhere. But then she married Bobby and stayed."

"And then he was murdered," Matt concluded.

Lynda nodded grimly.

"That still doesn't explain why me."

"I saw you that summer, the two of you," she said, surprising him. "Long before Ed found out and made a ruckus about the whole thing. I knew there was something between the two of you. I'd see you at the diner, the way you couldn't take your eyes off her, the little private smiles you shared, like you were all alone in a room full of people. And when I tried to think of somebody, anybody in this world who might care enough to help her, I remembered you."

"How did you find me?"

"I have a friend whose son does background checks for the state. It was easy enough. There are a lot of Matt Alvarezes out there, but I knew about what age you were. It was just a matter of tracking down the right one."

"Weren't you worried it would look bad, a guy she dated a long time ago showing up right after her husband was murdered?"

"I didn't believe it could get any worse. How could it? She already had the whole town against her, the police determined to prove she was guilty. What she needed was someone on her side."

"And you thought somebody she knew for a few months who'd been gone for eight years was the best person out of everybody in the world to be on her side?"

"No, I thought somebody who once loved her might still care enough not to want to see her in prison."

Loved her? Matt tried not to let his surprise show at the woman's words. And it was a surprise. Not that he'd loved Elena—he knew that, of course—but that anyone had known, especially someone he hadn't been aware of and hadn't spoken to before in his life. The way he and Elena had felt about each other had been private. He'd never told another soul, and other than perhaps her father when he'd tried tearing them apart, he didn't believe she had, either. It had been between them, theirs and theirs alone. But there wasn't the slightest doubt in this woman's voice. To hear her put it so simply, to find out that someone else had known came as a pure shock. "How did you—"

She eyed him knowingly. "I saw the way you looked

at her back then, the way she looked at you. You loved each other."

He couldn't deny it.

"What about Bobby Weston?" he asked before he could stop himself. "How'd she look at him?"

"Not the same way. I think she wanted to. It was like she was trying her best, but it wasn't the same."

The answer gave him no pleasure, imagining Elena unhappy like that. "And Weston?" he asked quietly. "Did he love her?"

A hint of sadness entered her eyes before she lowered them. "Yes," she said. "I believe he did. Certainly in the beginning. He looked at her the way she never looked at him."

It was the last thing Matt ever would have expected, but damned if he didn't feel a twinge of sympathy for the man. But then, he knew what it was like to love Elena more than anything, and to believe she didn't love him the same way. He wouldn't have wished that feeling on anybody, not even the man who'd gotten to marry her. And while he couldn't condone the way Bobby had treated her, he could understand it. Because he also knew what it was like to think he hated her. He couldn't imagine what it would have been like to be married to her, be around her every day, and feel that way. As much as he hated to admit it, he wasn't sure his behavior would have been any better.

Hell, he'd walked away from her, leaving her crying on the street. He really wasn't much better.

But he could still make it up to her.

No, he *would* make it up to her, he thought fiercely. Whatever he had to do, he'd make amends for ever having made her that unhappy.

"You love her."

Matt glanced up to find Lynda watching him, a small, sad smile on her lips.

His first impulse was to deny it. It was ridiculous. He really hadn't been carrying some kind of pathetic torch for Elena all these years.

But despite his intentions, the words never came.

Because it didn't matter what he'd thought, what he'd felt, when he'd first come back to town. It wasn't what he felt now.

He loved her. Just the thought of losing her again, in any way, sent a sharp, agonizing pain straight through his chest.

Lynda studied him, her smile deepening. "I was hoping you cared enough about her to not want to see her in jail, but I didn't know if there'd be any romantic feelings left." She leaned forward, her smile fading, a serious gleam in her eyes. "Whatever happens, don't let her go this time. Life's too short."

"You're right about that." He didn't tell her that he had no intention of letting Elena go again. The first person he intended to tell that was Elena herself.

He'd waited long enough.

Chapter Thirteen

After Matt left, Elena tried to focus on the work she had to do around the ranch. But no matter how much she tried to avoid it, her thoughts kept returning to the unexpected information he'd delivered about her mother.

Was it possible? Had her mother not left her after all? On the one hand, she supposed she should find that comforting in some way, that her mother hadn't abandoned her, hadn't rejected her as she'd always believed. But to suspect that something had happened to her instead, that she'd met with some terrible end, wasn't comforting at all. Elena wasn't sure if she should hope it was true, or if she shouldn't, or if she should do anything at all.

She hadn't arrived at any answers or found the slightest peace when she heard the vehicle coming up the driveway. Instantly going on alert, she immediately moved to the front door. A sigh of relief worked its way from her lungs once she saw who it was.

Matt. He was back.

Stepping out onto the porch, she watch him park out front. Once he had, he didn't get out of the truck immediately. Elena could tell he was looking at her, could feel the heat of his gaze on her. What was he doing?

Frowning, she waited for him to climb out and join her on the porch, her concern growing the longer he didn't.

She was considering walking down to the truck to check on him when he finally opened the door and slowly got out. He took his time gently closing the door behind himself, then made his way to her, his steps deliberate, his head lowered slightly as though he were deep in thought. She felt her unease build. He looked as though he was carrying the weight of the world on his shoulders.

Matt finally reached the steps, moving up them until he stood on the porch with her.

"Is everything all right?" she asked carefully.

"Yeah," he said simply.

The vague answer did nothing to put her mind at ease. "Did you talk to Jack?"

Matt nodded. "Didn't get anything out of him. He denied everything, of course."

"No surprise there."

"I also talked to Lynda Clayton. She was the one who sent me the article about you."

"Lynda Clayton?" she blurted out. She knew who the woman was, of course. That didn't mean the words made any sense. She couldn't remember the last time she'd even spoken to the woman, or frankly if she really had.

He nodded. "She was friends with your mother growing up," he explained. "Best friends, the way she tells it. Sounds like she married up and your mother married down, and she kind of cut your mother loose. After your mother…left…" He glanced away awkwardly, lingering on the word in a way that made it clear he wasn't entirely comfortable putting it like that and reminding her rather painfully of their earlier conversation. "Well, she felt bad for the way she treated her and tried to keep an eye on you. Sounds like she's been looking out for you in various ways over the years. After the murder she figured you might need more help than she could give and…well, here I am."

For the second time in one day he'd managed to completely throw her for a loop, delivering new information she didn't know how to process. First her mother may not have left them, may have had something happen to her. Now Lynda Clayton, a woman who she would have thought was only marginally aware of her existence, had been looking out for her?

Elena had had no idea Lynda and her mother had been friends. But then, her father had barely spoken of her, and never much in the way of personal details. No one else really had, either. There was so little she knew about Teresa Reyes, her friends, the life she'd led. She only knew that she'd left.

And now maybe she didn't even know that.

Shaking her head, she opened her mouth to question him further when she realized he was staring at her, his eyes haunted, his expression pained. The sight of his expression filled her with fresh apprehension. It seemed he was nervous to tell her something. She braced herself, wondering what more there could possibly be.

He finally spoke. "I'm sorry."

"For what?"

"For eight years ago. For…expecting you to give up all your plans to follow some cowboy without a job God knows where. That wasn't fair to you. I was wrong. You deserved better than that."

The words stunned her into silence. She'd never expected to hear them, had no idea what had brought them about, didn't know how to begin to respond.

"You were never just some cowboy," she whispered, the words coming automatically.

It was what she'd tried to tell him before, that he'd never been just anybody to her. This time he didn't blow the comment off, a pained look flashing across his face. "Still, it wasn't right. I knew it was no kind of life for you. I shouldn't have gotten so mad." He swallowed, his voice softening. "I shouldn't have walked away from you."

"It's okay. I understood why. I'm sorry. I wish I'd been able to come with you, strong enough to take the chance. If I'd known how things would turn out…"

He stepped forward, moving so achingly close to her. "Don't," he said. "You can't do that to yourself. We never know what's going to happen. The time just wasn't right for us."

Maybe it was as simple as that, she acknowledged as she peered up into his eyes. Maybe no one had been at fault. They'd wanted different things, different lives. And at that time there'd simply been no way for them to work.

"And now?" she whispered.

"I don't know if it's the right time. I just know I don't want to let you go again."

"Then don't." The words caught in her throat, practically coming out on a sob, filled with every ounce of feeling she was experiencing, every soul-deep need.

Don't let me go.

She didn't have to say anything more. He reached out and took her in his arms.

A lump rose in her throat, and she pressed her lips

together against the sob she was certain would come out if she opened her mouth. She'd missed this, hadn't realized just how much she'd needed it until now. To feel his arms around her. To feel him holding her, simply holding her, so very close. It was just as she remembered. His arms felt different, his body harder, more muscular, after all these years. It didn't matter. She recognized the feel of his embrace as well as if he'd never let her go.

It felt like coming home.

They simply clung to each other, and at first it was enough. This was all she needed. But gradually she began to soak in the heat of his body, his warmth seeping through the layers of clothing and into her skin. Like a slow-acting drug, it spread through her from head to toe, filling her to the core with his heat. The first flickers of awareness sparked to life deep in her belly, the stirrings of arousal building in strength and power. Each moment brought awareness of something new, each fresh discovery adding fuel to the fire. The broad muscularity of his chest beneath her cheek. The strength of his back beneath her fingers and palms. His intoxicating male scent filling her lungs. And she knew she had to have more.

She wanted him, as much as she ever had before, if not more.

As if realizing it exactly at the same time, he eased his hold on her and leaned back slightly. Elena raised her head from his chest and tilted it back to meet his eyes. The dark heat she saw burning in those black depths made it clear she wasn't alone in feeling what she was. Even the sight of it there pushed her awareness, her need, higher.

Then he slowly lowered his mouth to hers.

He kissed her softly, sweetly, with a gentleness that drove a sigh from deep in her throat. His warm, sensual lips stroked against hers, tasting, inviting them to open for him. She responded in kind, deepening the kiss with each subsequent caress. His tongue pushed forward, finding hers, teasing lightly, retreating, then finding it again. A chuckle rumbled deep in her chest at the joy of it, giddy delight bubbling up inside her. She'd forgotten how much fun kissing him could be. It was heady and arousing, but also playful and joyous. He continually surprised her, made it interesting, kept her on her toes, which only made it more exciting.

He broke away to work a trail of kisses along her jaw and down her neck. She automatically leaned her head away to allow him easier access, savoring each lap of his tongue, each brush of his lips against her soft skin.

Her eyes drifted open for just a moment, allowing her to see where they were. Out in the open where anyone could see. More important, on the porch of the house that had never really been hers, where generations of Westons had lived before. The realization immediately diminished her fire slightly. Instinctively knowing where this was heading, where she wanted it to go, she knew she couldn't do this here. They needed to go someplace that was hers and hers alone as much as anyplace in the world was.

She moved her mouth to his ear. "Let's go upstairs," she whispered.

He lifted his head to look into her face. "You sure?"

"Yes." She couldn't recall ever being as sure of anything in her life.

One corner of his mouth moving upward in a slow,

sensual smile, Matt released his hold on her. Reaching down, she took his hand and pulled him inside.

They made it to her bedroom, Elena stepping in first, when he suddenly stopped, his resistance bringing her to a halt, too. She glanced back to find him standing just outside the doorway, eyeing the room with a distinct sense of unease.

"Did you and…"

Elena understood immediately. She shook her head. "This is my room. I moved in here once things got too broken between us. We stopped sharing a bed—in any way."

Matt nodded, both relief and a trace of apology in his eyes. It wasn't what she wanted to see there. She wanted the dark heat back in them, wanted him to look at her with that raw fire that said he wanted to devour her.

She wanted him. Wanted him with far fewer clothes for starters.

Moving toward him, she reached for the buttons on his shirt. Popping the first one, she murmured, "Any more questions?"

She sensed his smile. "Nope."

"Good," she said, continuing to release the buttons, pulling him farther into the room by his shirt. She didn't want this to go too fast, needing to take in every moment, every part of the experience. So long. It had been so long since she'd seen his body, since she'd touched his skin, since she'd felt every part of him. She'd never thought she would again. She wanted to relish it, bask in every sensation. She finally finished with the buttons and opened his shirt, revealing his long, lean torso to her. A breath caught in her throat as she simply looked at first, at his firm musculature, his flat belly, his smooth bronze skin. He'd gotten bigger, stronger. He was still the most beautiful man she'd ever seen.

When she started to push the shirt from his shoulders, Matt pulled the gun from the waistband of his jeans and placed it on the bedside table, then turned back to her.

They undressed each other together, taking their time, moving slowly, working together. Boots were tugged off, buttons were released, fabric slid from shoulders and arms. All the while, they touched and explored, as if amazed by every next bit of flesh that was revealed. Which she was. She knew his body so well, the line of his shoulders, the length of his torso. It was all so familiar, yet so different at the same time, leaner in some places, more muscular in others. She could only imagine he felt the same, as his fingers stroked her breasts, her belly, her hips. She knew her body was different than it had been. She'd gotten older, rounder in places. A trace of anxiety flickered through her. She hoped he liked what he saw.

One glance at his face, his eyes unerringly focused on her, said he did.

Finally, there was nothing else covering them and they stood bare before each other. His hands trailed along her sides as he stepped forward and kissed her once more. They almost immediately deepened it together. His arms went around her, his hands finding her hips and lifting her off her feet. Her breasts pressed against the hard wall of his chest, the heat of his skin burning against her own. She wound her arms around his neck as he stepped forward, carrying her to the bed. There was a sound when his legs hit the edge of it. Then he was lowering her onto it, easing her on the mattress, stretching out beside her.

As his hands moved over her body, his mouth over hers, it struck her that they'd never done this before, never made love in an actual bed. Back then, they'd had to find a place together wherever they could, and a bed had never entered the equation. Instead, they'd made love in the bed of his truck, parked in an isolated, out-of-the-way spot, or on a blanket spread out under the stars. They'd certainly never lacked for not having been in a bed. Wherever they'd been, it had been lovely. All they'd needed was each other.

But still, it was nice to be in a bed this time. It was like a new experience for them, as if it were their first time. And it was, their first time since they'd found each other again. It seemed right somehow.

They took their time exploring each other's bodies, until it wasn't enough. He rolled away and reached for his wallet, pulling a packet from it and covering himself. Then he came back to her.

Elena parted her legs, letting him move between them, wanting him there. Matt positioned himself above her and leaned forward to kiss her again. She breathed in the experience of it, basking in the weight of him above her and between her legs. The tip of his erection nudged insistently against her folds, as though asking for admission. She was more than ready. And when Matt finally thrust into her, she raised her hips to meet him.

The breath caught in her throat as they remained there for an instant, locked together. It was so right. She smiled, unable to believe she'd existed without this, without him for so long, that giddy joy spiraling through her. He smiled back at her, that gorgeous smile he offered far too rarely, that the world seldom got to see. Her heart felt on the verge of bursting, from this moment, from this man, from the beauty of his smile.

They began moving together in perfect rhythm, hips moving apart, finding each other again. Elena wrapped her arms around his neck again, unable to get enough of touching him, needing to feel as much of him as possible. Bracing himself above her on his arms, he drove into her, harder, faster, pushing her to greater, seemingly impossible heights. She stared up into his eyes, watching his face, the emotions flashing across it, the pleasure. As she came closer and closer to the edge, she saw him approach it with her, the tension building in his face, his neck and shoulders. And when she reached it, he was right there with her, looking deep in her eyes at the moment of their release.

And as the waves of her release ebbed away, they left amazement in their wake. Amazement at the rightness of this moment, of having found each other again, of a new beginning she'd never dreamed possible.

Yet here it was.

Here *he* was, back where he belonged.

With her.

Chapter Fourteen

Matt woke to darkness.

Drifting awake, he slowly peeled his eyelids open to peer into the shadows above him. It was night, he registered. The ceiling above him was unfamiliar. So was the bed.

Still, he didn't have to look to see where he was. He knew. He recognized the feel of the woman at his side, the sweet smell that was uniquely hers, as a deep, warm contentment spread through him at the knowledge.

He was with Elena. Where he belonged. There was nowhere else he ever wanted to be.

His mouth curving in a smile, he lay there and simply basked in the feeling, better than anything he'd ever known. He couldn't remember the last time he'd ever been this happy. Maybe not since they'd parted ways before, maybe never at all. He breathed in the scent of her, absorbed the thump of her heartbeat from where her body was pressed against him, listened to the soft sound of her breathing.

He didn't know how he'd survived without this, without her, all this time. He only knew that he couldn't again. God willing, he would never have to.

He would have loved nothing more than to remain

where he was, closing his eyes and drifting back to sleep with this amazing woman curled up beside him. But even as he started to do so, he remembered what had happened last night, and the night before.

He opened his eyes fully once more. It had still been early evening then. Judging from the darkness, it was now much later, well into the night. The time their nasty visitor liked to come out and play.

Hard determination replaced the contentment that had filled him just moments before.

He was going to catch the bastard. He wasn't getting away with anything tonight.

He should do a check of the grounds. At the very least, he should make sure the house was secure. He couldn't remember if they'd locked any of the doors, and it was worth checking out. Their troublemaker had been getting bolder. He'd feel a lot better if he knew more definitively that they were safe.

Swallowing a sigh of regret, he eased himself from the bed and quickly dressed. Sitting down to tug his boots on, he glanced back at Elena. The sight of her there, curled up on her side facing him, nearly cracked his resolve and made him crawl back in beside her.

Soon. He'd be back soon enough. In the meantime, he had work to do.

He retrieved the gun he'd placed on the bedside table, keeping it in hand. With one last, lingering look, he headed downstairs.

The house was still and quiet. His footsteps as silent as possible on the hardwood floor, he kept his ears peeled for the slightest noise, the faintest disturbance. He detected nothing as he made his way down the stairs to the front.

He stopped at the front door, checking the lock, giving a perfunctory glance outside through the window. So perfunctory he almost missed seeing it, the shadow at the edge of the barn moving toward the house.

He'd been about to turn away from the door. Instead, he froze, eyes returning to the figure as it crept forward, trying to remain in darkness as much as possible. The figure was dressed in black, a ski mask covering his face.

Triumph surged from deep in Matt's gut. This was it. He was going to get the guy.

Not about to wait and see what the bastard had in mind, to miss the chance to catch him, Matt quickly considered his options. If he went out the kitchen door and circled around the back, he should be able to get the drop on the person.

But only if he moved quickly.

As soon as he thought it, he sprang into motion, bursting away from the door and racing through the house on the balls of his feet to the back.

Reaching the kitchen door, he slowly pulled it open, careful not to make a sound. When he had it open just wide enough for him to pass through, he slipped through the gap and hurried outside.

It took him less than thirty seconds to make his way around the side of the house to the front. He paused at the corner, carefully looking around the edge to scan for the trespasser.

He instantly spotted him, standing almost in front of the house. The man was looking down, something clutched in his right hand. A glass bottle. In his left he held a lighter, which he started to ignite. Once he had a flame he started lifting it to something dangling out of the mouth of the bottle—

Recognition slammed into Matt.

It was a fire bomb. Which could only mean one thing.

He was planning on throwing it into the house.

No.

Without a second thought, Matt burst from the shadows and charged the bastard, automatically shoving the gun into the back of his waistband with one hand, fighting to outrace the rag's ignition. At the last second the trespasser must have spotted the motion out of the corner of his eye, jerking his head up in Matt's direction.

Too late to do anything about it.

Matt crashed into him, locking his arms around the trespasser and knocking him clear off his feet. In the back of his mind, he heard the bottle the man had been holding crash to the ground and break into pieces. The smell of gasoline filled the air.

They landed hard on the ground, rolling away from the odor, tumbling against the packed dirt. The man started to fight him, throwing his arms and knees and his body weight against Matt as best he could. The bastard was strong as hell, Matt had to give him that. Matt fought to keep a hold on him. He finally managed to get on top of the intruder, straddling him with his legs. He pulled back long enough to draw a fist, driving it hard into the man's masked face. The punch was enough to get the bastard to stop struggling for an instant. Matt drew his fist back again and landed another blow, making the man weaken further. Matt wasted no more time, reaching for the gun he'd shoved at the small of his back and aiming it directly between the intruder's eyes.

"Stop it," Matt ordered when the man would have started fighting back again. He cocked the weapon, drawing the intruder's attention. The bastard froze, eyes slowly focusing on the barrel of the gun less than six inches from his face.

Matt read the calculation in those narrowed eyes. "Go ahead," he said, satisfaction pulsing through his veins. "You don't know how badly I want to pull the trigger."

They stared at each other for a long moment, locked in a silent battle of wills. There was no way Matt was going to blink first.

Finally, the other man relaxed slightly, his eyes reflecting his acknowledgment that he'd been bested—and fury that he had been.

Matt barely restrained a triumphant grin. This wasn't the time to get cocky. Remembering their battle the night before, he knew how quickly the balance could change. "Now let's see who the hell you are."

Reaching down with his free hand, he ripped the mask off, baring the man's face. He wasn't at all surprised at what he saw.

As expected, Deputy Travis Gerard glared back at him, his expression mutinous, unrepentant.

It was all Matt could do not to drive his fist into the deputy's arrogant face one more time. "I should have known you were behind this, you bastard," he forced out, his jaw tight. Keeping the gun steady, Matt slowly rose, never shifting his aim. Travis never took his eyes from the gun, either.

When Matt was on his feet, he took a couple steps back and away from the man. "Get up," he ordered.

From the look Travis shot him he was tempted to defy the order just for the hell of it. But he gradually climbed to his feet, taking his time, making a big show of it. When he finally straightened, he brushed some of the dirt off his clothes and stood facing Matt, meeting his eyes.

Matt stared back, his sense of victory quickly dimming as he considered the reality of the situation at hand. Because he hadn't just caught someone committing a crime on private property. He'd caught a sheriff's deputy doing it. A sheriff's deputy in a department that wasn't going to be inclined to believe anything Matt had to say, that would probably have no problem with his actions or with covering them up.

"So what the hell are you going to do now?" Travis snapped, regaining some of his bravado.

That was the problem. "I haven't decided," he said coldly. "If I call the sheriff, he's not going to believe me, is he? He'll somehow turn this around on me, probably charge me with assaulting an officer and let you off scot-free, won't he?" And if he got arrested, Elena would be alone out here, openly vulnerable to whatever attack Travis decided to launch next. Which he would, of course. If he got away with this there'd be nothing holding him back from trying again.

Travis's smirk said he shared Matt's analysis—and fully expected everything to unfold as described.

At the sight of the man's smugness, Matt saw red, nearly hitting his breaking point with this dirtbag and this whole situation. In an instant, all he wanted was to see the bastard squirm.

"Hell, I might as well shoot you then," Matt said, gratified to see the smirk slowly fade from Travis's mouth. "If I do, then there's no way he can turn this around on me. We have you dressed all in black, trespassing here in the middle of the night. I could always claim I didn't know who you were. Nobody could blame me for shooting some guy who was getting ready to throw a firebomb into the house."

"You wouldn't," Travis challenged, not looking entirely sure about that. "You'd never get away with it."

"I should," Matt said. "It's what you deserve. A firebomb? What the hell were you thinking? She could have been killed!" Travis simply stared back at him, as if Matt wasn't telling him anything he didn't already know, or something he couldn't care less about. "Did you slash her tires in town, too?"

He said nothing, his mouth a tight line, but the glint in his eye looked too much like pride.

"You bastard. Do you have any idea what you've put her through?"

"Good. It's what she deserves."

"What the hell do you want from her?"

"I want her to confess! I want her to admit what she did. Until she does she doesn't deserve a moment's peace. She doesn't deserve to have a good night's rest in this house that she damn well doesn't deserve to own."

In the wake of his outburst, Travis stood there, chest heaving, face mottled with emotion. But there was more than anger in the man's words. There was pain, in his face, in his voice, almost like he was on the verge of tears. The man truly believed Elena killed his best friend, practically his brother, Matt acknowledged. He could understand the man's motives, even if he damn well couldn't condone his actions.

The best he could do was try to come to some kind of understanding, some way to get him to back off.

"All right. I'm going to tell you this once, Gerard. The sooner you realize this, the sooner you can start figuring out who's really responsible. Elena did not kill Bobby."

"Then who the hell did?"

"Maybe if you opened your damn mind and even considered the possibility that someone else is responsible you'd figure it out."

"You think I haven't? You think I haven't considered every single person in this town, thought of every possible reason any one of them would have killed Bobby? I haven't come up with a damn thing. The only person with a reason, the only person who could have done it is *her*."

"Just because you haven't found the answer yet doesn't mean it's not there."

"Or else I've already found it."

"Damn it, Gerard. I can promise you, Elena didn't kill him."

"And how do you know that, huh?"

"Because I know her. And you should, too. You should know she's no killer."

"Yeah, I know her," he scoffed. "I know she's a gold digger who trapped a good man into marrying her when she didn't even love him. It took him a while to realize it, but Bobby knew it. It used to eat him up. She didn't love him. He just didn't know that she was hung up on somebody else. It was you, wasn't it? All this time. And now you come back here the minute he's dead, sleeping in his house, with his wife—"

· "It's not like that—" Matt began.

"The hell it's not!" Travis said. "So don't tell me she didn't do it. You don't tell me a damn thing, because I sure as hell don't believe a word you say."

They stood there glaring at each other in the moonlight. It hardly mattered that Travis didn't want to hear what he had to say, because Matt didn't know what he even could say. If he were in Travis's shoes he'd probably feel the same way about things. Short of finding the real killer, there wasn't going to be any convincing him Elena was innocent. And as for the rest… No, Travis wasn't likely to believe them about any of that, either.

That didn't mean Matt was going to put up with any more of the man's garbage. He probably couldn't count on the sheriff to do anything to stop him, which meant he was going to have to find some way—

His only warning came a split second before it happened. Travis's gaze abruptly moved behind him, his eyes widening slightly in response to what he saw.

Matt didn't have time to react.

Then he couldn't.

A split second later, something heavy crashed into the back of his head. His vision blurred and he stumbled forward. He tried to regain his balance as the world seemed to swim around him and his feet seemed to have disappeared. Then he was falling, falling endlessly. Until…

Nothing.

SOMETHING WOKE HER.

Something loud, a noise of some kind. It prodded her

to wakefulness, pushing her from the best sleep she'd had in a long time.

Still half-asleep, Elena registered that she was cold. A source of warmth she'd gotten used to wasn't there anymore. Matt.

Without opening her eyes, she reached out to find him.

And found only cold sheets.

She opened her eyes to glance at where Matt had been lying at her side.

His half of the bed was empty. He was gone.

Frowning, she slowly sat up, more confused than concerned. "Matt?"

The sound of her voice echoing through the open doorway and down the hall emphasized the emptiness of the house and the sense that she truly was alone.

No answer.

She glanced toward the window, noting the darkness outside. It was the dead of night.

The trouble they'd had the past couple nights suddenly came rushing back to her. Had something happened? Had he heard a noise? Their troublemaker again? Why wouldn't he have woken her?

No, if he'd heard something he would have woken her, wouldn't he? He wouldn't have simply left her alone and helpless in bed.

Everything was probably fine.

Still, she couldn't quite shake the feeling of unease crawling along her nerve endings. The house was so quiet. Too quiet. And there'd been that noise, she remembered, trying to place it, trying to recall what it could have been.

Climbing from the bed, she reached for her clothes

and quickly tugged them on, then moved to the window. Standing to the side of it, she gently pulled the curtain back an inch, then leaned over and peered out.

Everything appeared to be still. It was a cloudy night, the moon and most of the stars hidden from view behind the dense coverage. It made the darkness more opaque that usual. Some light from the house spilled out into the yard and driveway, and the light fixed on the post next to the barn did its job illuminating most of the area directly in front of it. But there seemed to be far more shadows than usual, stretching across the ground, keeping much of it in darkness. She couldn't see much out there, except—

It took her a moment to understand what it was she was seeing. And then—

A gasp lodged in her throat.

A man lay on the ground in front of the house.

Everything inside her tensed in shock, in horror.

No.

He wasn't visible enough for her to make him out much, just out of range of the big light out front, hidden in the shadows on the edge of the driveway. She couldn't see his face, couldn't really make out his clothes. She only saw a silhouette, the figure large enough it looked like a man to her.

Had the intruder come back? Had he done something to Matt?

She tried to peer closer, desperate for any indication it was Matt. But if it wasn't, where was he?

Whether or not it was Matt, something must be wrong. There was no reason for someone to simply be lying there on the ground unless he was hurt…or dead.

She shoved the thought aside. She couldn't afford to think like that. She had to figure out what to do.

She could call the police, but somehow she doubted Walt or Travis would rush out here, even if they did believe her. And in the meantime, Matt could be dying.

The hell if she was going to cower in her house while the man she loved was out there, possibly on the verge of drawing his last breath.

Moving back to her bedside table, Elena retrieved her gun, not about to go out there unarmed. And this time, if there were someone who meant her harm, who'd done something to Matt, she wouldn't be firing into the air.

When she reached the bedroom door, she was about to step out into the hall when she paused, thinking quickly. If someone had gotten to Matt, there was a chance they'd already managed to get inside the house.

They could be here now, coming for her.

Holding her pistol up in front of her, she slowly eased her head through the door frame, looking down the hall to the stairs.

Nothing. The hall was clear.

Not about to take it for granted that would continue to be the case, Elena quickly and silently moved into the hall, her gun poised and ready to be aimed at the slightest sign of motion. She headed for the stairs, checking open doorways along the way, then made her way down to the first level. Nothing stirred. Keeping her breathing as silent as possible, she didn't hear a single sound in the house or from outside. The quiet only made her more nervous. It was almost *too* quiet, unnervingly so.

At the bottom of the stairs, the front door beckoned to her. She ignored it. She couldn't go out the front. It was too open; she'd be entirely exposed. Not to mention this could be a trap. Someone could be trying to lure her out of the house, and if so, they'd likely be waiting out there, maybe even by one of the sides of the door, waiting for her to open it, ready to ambush her. She had no choice but to go out there—as long as there was a chance that Matt was vulnerable, hurt, she had to do something—but if this were a trap, she was going to do her best to avoid it. She'd go out the back, stick to the darkness along the side of the house. While there might be someone out there, it would give her the best chance to remain as unseen as possible.

Once she had a plan, she executed it quickly, hurrying to the kitchen. The door was already slightly ajar, drawing her to a halt. What did that mean? *Was* there someone in the house?

If so, that was more reason than ever to get out.

Moving to the open doorway, she pressed herself against the wall and looked out. There was no one lying in wait, at least not on that side. They could still be on the other.

Only one way to find out.

Taking a breath, she raised the gun next to her head, then reached for the doorknob.

One…two…

Three.

She whipped the door open, jumping out and aiming her weapon at the side she'd been unable to check.

Nothing. There was no one there.

She didn't waste time letting relief sink in, instantly moving forward and around the house.

When she made it to the front, she stopped at the corner, her eyes immediately going to the spot where she'd seen the man. It took her a few seconds to make him out, but he was there, exactly where he'd been before. She quashed every instinct that wanted to rush to his side. That was exactly what she couldn't do, of course.

Instead, she moved forward slowly, carefully making her way to the figure, keeping her head moving and her eyes shifting in every direction at all times, not about to let anyone sneak up on her.

All the while, she kept glancing back at the man, constantly checking if she could make out his face, her heart climbing higher and higher in her throat the closer and closer she came.

And then she was there. Close enough. She saw his face.

She lurched to a stop, the shock of it too great to let her feel any relief.

The man on the ground wasn't Matt.

No. It was Travis.

Travis, dressed entirely in black, lay on the ground. Travis, unblinking, stared sightlessly up at the sky.

Travis, mouth agape with horror, had a hole in the middle of his forehead.

A gunshot, she realized, staring in disbelief at the horrible sight. That must have been what woke her. She'd heard the gunshot. But who could have done this? And where was Matt—

"Drop it," a voice ordered behind her, snapping her out of her daze. The command was punctuated by the sound of a weapon being cocked.

The voice sent relief rushing through her, because she recognized it too well.

Oh, thank God.

"I said drop it," the man repeated, the voice unmistakably that of Sheriff Walt Bremer.

She opened her fingers and let the pistol tumble from it.

He slowly shifted in front of her, allowing her to see she hadn't been mistaken.

"Don't move," he ordered. With one quick motion, he kicked the gun away. Keeping both his eyes and his weapon on her at all times, Walt slowly moved to where he'd kicked the gun, then bent to retrieve it, shoving it into the back of his waistband.

His eyes glittered with coldness and…something else.

He reached down to his belt with his free hand, grabbed a pair of handcuffs, then threw them at her feet. "Put those on."

Her relief instantly died, replaced with fresh fear. His deputy was dead. Walt already thought she'd killed Bobby. He probably thought she'd killed Travis, too.

"I didn't do this," she said quickly but firmly.

Walt simply gestured toward the cuffs with a jut of his chin. "Put 'em on."

There didn't seem to be any point in arguing, not with that look in his eyes, not with the gun he kept on her with unwavering focus. Heck, he might just be looking for a reason to pull the trigger. She definitely wouldn't be able to defend herself if she was dead.

She bent down to retrieve the cuffs, moving slowly to demonstrate she wasn't going to try anything and wasn't a threat. The metal was cold in her hands. She carefully locked one cuff around her left wrist, then moved to fasten the other.

"Tighter," he barked out.

Biting her tongue, she complied, squeezing the cuffs until they were taut against her wrists, yet not tight enough to dig into her skin. That didn't make them feel any less unbearable. She'd imagined the moment Walt would take her away in cuffs, of course, the image haunting her. But never had she pictured it like this. And, of course, she'd imagined Travis would be there in an entirely different context, grinning smugly the whole way.

"I didn't shoot Travis," Elena tried again.

One corner of his mouth tilted upward in a humorless smile. "Sure you did, Elena. You and your boyfriend. It's the only explanation. Travis here had the two of you under surveillance. He saw you were about to run and tried to stop you. The two of you got away. It's clear as day. Nobody will have any trouble believing it."

The straightforward way he laid it out made it seem eminently reasonable. Listening to him tell it, she almost might have believed it, too. Except for one thing.

"But I didn't get away," she pointed out, even as a warning bell was clanging in the back of her mind, even as the puzzle pieces were clicking into place and she understood that she was in even more trouble than she'd imagined. "I'm still here."

"Are you?" Walt simply smiled, as though they were sharing a private joke, or maybe he was telling one and waiting for her to get the punchline. Which she already had, she acknowledged, as she realized what she'd deduced had to be true.

This was bad. So very bad.

Because the only thing worse than Walt believing she was guilty of a second murder…

Was if he was the killer himself.

Chapter Fifteen

"*You* killed Travis."

There was no need to say it. She already knew it was true. It was the only possible explanation, the only thing that made any sense. Except it didn't make sense, not at all. Part of her really did need him to confirm it, that this was really happening.

Walt smirked. "Why would I do something like that?"

"You tell me," she shot back, desperately needing him to, desperately needing to understand any of this.

The smirk didn't fade, but there was still a perceptible change in his demeanor, his expression hardening, his eyes growing colder. "It's time to end this. I've waited long enough."

"For what?"

His expression barely changed, but something in the way he looked at her made her skin crawl. "You'll find out soon enough."

He was clearly insane. She couldn't believe he'd simply murdered Travis like that in cold blood.

No, not just Travis, she suddenly knew, the knowledge hitting her hard. He must have also—

"You killed Bobby."

He raised one shoulder and tipped his head slightly, as if it were nothing. The gesture was so infuriatingly casual her anger spiked.

"Why?" she demanded.

He shook his head. "Bobby had that damn fool idea about digging up the back of the spread. I couldn't let him do that. I couldn't let him dig up what's out there."

That was what this was all about? "What's out there?"

"Souvenirs. Big Jim was a fool, too, liked to keep his women close. Buried them on his own damn property. Of course, he never thought anyone would be digging out there. He certainly didn't count on dying as young as he did."

Souvenirs? Women? Buried on the property? It felt as if he was talking in riddles. She wished he would just cut to the chase and spill it already.

Only one thing was clear enough. Walt had killed Bobby. He was behind all of this.

Which still didn't make any sense. She thought of the reason she'd dismissed him as a possible suspect. "I don't understand. If you killed Bobby, you must have had the murder weapon the whole time. Why not just plant it and arrest me?"

"Because I didn't want to arrest you. I just wanted you to look guilty enough that everybody would believe you ran to escape justice when you disappeared."

"Disappeared?" she echoed faintly.

Still smiling, his eyes stroked over her, trailing down her body with a thoroughness and such open interest she went cold from head to toe. "I've been waiting for this for a long time."

Oh, God. "Waiting for what?" she said warily, fearing she already knew.

"You're a beautiful woman, Elena. Grew up real nice. Your mother was beautiful, too. You look a lot like her."

It didn't occur to her to question why he was bringing up her mother. She automatically knew. He was talking about making her disappear. Her mother had disappeared, no one questioning that she'd run away. And Elena knew, the realization hitting her like a blow straight to the gut.

"My mother didn't run away. You killed her." And not just her, Elena knew, her horror growing. The other women who'd gone missing, possibly victims of a serial killer.

Big Jim's women. His souvenirs. Buried out in the back of the spread.

So that was it. What Walt had been worried Bobby would dig up. The reason he'd had to die.

His smile deepened, the sight piercing her numbness and filling her with sudden rage. "She was so beautiful," he said wistfully, his gaze growing dreamy and distant. "Normally we wouldn't have taken someone so close to home, someone we knew, someone we knew had people who would miss her. But she was just so beautiful. Jim wanted her bad. So did I. Finally, we just had to have her."

He lapsed into silence, not elaborating on what had happened then. He didn't have to, as Elena saw his smile, the gleam in his eye, the sheer grotesque happiness he displayed as he remembered. Elena felt bile rise in her throat and nearly gagged, from horror, from revulsion, at the idea of what must have been done to her mother at those men's hands.

For just a moment, guilt surged from the pit of her stomach, washing over her, nearly overwhelming her. She'd spent practically her whole life hating her mother, believing she'd left them, left *her*. And she'd been dead the whole time, taken away by this monster.

This monster who now wanted her.

The reminder brought her crashing back to reality. She was the one now facing those same dire straits her mother once had. She had no trouble believing Walt was capable of making it look like she'd run away. He'd done it before.

But not before he did God only knew to her.

The hell he will.

Everything within her rejected the idea, a fierce determination gripping her. Teresa Reyes couldn't have known what would happen to her beforehand. Most of the other women probably didn't, either. But Elena did, and she damn well wasn't going down without a fight.

If there was any outward change in her demeanor, Walt didn't react to it. His gaze remained far away, that despicable smile on his face. Elena wondered if it would be possible to make a move while his attention was elsewhere, distracted by his own disgusting thoughts. Maybe she could go for the gun—

Whether she tensed or he simply realized he'd let his mind wander too long, Walt suddenly sharpened his focus, his eyes narrowing on her face, the gun centering on her chest.

"And now it's time for you to go," he said.

"Do you really expect me to just go with you willingly, knowing what you intend to do to me?"

"I think you will. Because if you don't cooperate, I'll kill your boyfriend."

Matt. Fresh shock rolled through her. It seemed impossible, but somehow, in the midst of processing the truth about Walt, about her mother, she'd forgotten about him.

"Where's Matt?"

Walt waved with his free hand. "Right over there."

Elena whipped her head in the direction he indicated.

It took her a moment to spot him in the dark. Once she finally saw him, she nearly shuddered with relief. He was lying on his side, facing her, his arms bound behind his back. She tried to see if he was injured, still breathing—

His eyelids suddenly popped open, his gaze meeting hers.

His eyes weren't easily visible in the dark, but she could make them out, his stare direct and purposeful. He glanced toward Walt, then back at her. She quickly interpreted the silent message he was sending her.

Keep him talking.

Of course. He was trying to come up with a plan. Maybe he could manage to sneak up on him as long as Walt didn't know he was still awake, or provide some kind of distraction allowing her to act.

She quickly turned back to Walt. "Is that supposed to be an incentive? Obviously you're planning on killing him anyway."

"Yes, but you want me to delay as long as possible, don't you? The longer I put it off, there's still a chance he can escape, make some big move and save you both, isn't there?" His tone was plainly mocking, making it clear how likely he thought that would be. "That's what he's doing over there, isn't he? Trying to come up with a plan?" He turned slightly as though to include Matt in the conversation. "I know you're conscious, Alvarez. Good. Let's get this over with."

"What over with?" Elena asked.

"We're getting out of here."

"And going where?"

"You'll find out soon enough." His voice hardened. "Alvarez, I said get up."

After a moment, Matt slowly rose to his feet, no easy task with the use of his arms restricted. He still managed it, keeping his head high and proud, staring down Walt the entire way.

If Walt was at all intimidated, he didn't show it. But then, he was the one with the gun. He jerked his head toward the side. "Come on, the both of you. I had to park far enough away from the house that no one would hear me approach, and I have no intention of carrying you both. Walk."

"And if we refuse?" Matt asked.

"If one of you refuses I'll shoot the other. Nowhere that'll prevent you from walking, but enough that it'll hurt like hell. Shoulder wounds aren't much fun. If you both refuse, you both get shot. Easy as that."

"You won't get away with this," Matt pressed. "I have a contact with the FBI I've been in touch with throughout this. She knows Elena is innocent and she'll know we haven't run. If anything happens to us, she'll be down here in no time, investigating our disappearances."

His eyes narrowed with suspicion, Walt surveyed Matt carefully. "Even if I believe you really do know someone with the FBI, it won't make any difference.

Let her look all she wants. She won't find a trace of you. This isn't my first time. I know how to set up a disappearance and get rid of a body so it won't be found. The FBI's come looking around before and they didn't find a thing. She won't, either."

"Technology's a lot more advanced than it was twenty-five years ago," Elena pointed out. "They have new ways of finding people, bodies. You don't think there's a chance they won't poke around the ranch, maybe find those bodies Big Jim has buried out there?"

"They're not going to dig up the whole ranch on some damn scavenger hunt. I'll take my chances."

"Then what?" she asked. "With Bobby dead and nobody left to carry out his irrigation plan, are you just going to leave those bodies out there?"

"I'll move the bodies soon enough. Should have done it years ago. As soon as enough time has passed and nobody's poking around, I'll take care of it. After you're gone, it'll take some time before the ranch's ownership is settled. It should be vacant for a while. I'll be able to take care of what's out there without anyone noticing."

"Even if you can make it look like we ran, my friend at the FBI isn't going to believe we shot a deputy before running," Matt said.

"Really? Even when Travis was clearly out of control and threatening Elena here? It seems pretty obvious things just got out of hand. Enough people knew what Travis was doing. Now here he is, dressed all in black, the remains of a homemade Molotov cocktail with his fingerprints on it nearby. Anyone can see what he came here to do. You stopped him, there was a struggle, and he got shot. Killing a sheriff's deputy in Texas? That's not something anybody's going to take lightly, no matter the reason. You had to know you were looking at a heap of trouble, and Elena already had enough of her own. It only makes sense you'd run."

The scary thing was, it did make sense hearing him explain it, as he was no doubt prepared to do after they "disappeared" and he had to present this version of events as fact.

"I don't understand," Elena said. "Why did you kill Travis?"

"He was always going to have to die. He was too hell-bent on seeing you pay. Once you disappeared, he would never have stopped trying to track you down, and when the trail got too cold, he might just realize how suspicious that was, might start asking questions. No, he served his purpose, setting up the events that everybody would believe made you run. There wasn't much further damage he could do, not after this. It was time to end this."

She wasn't surprised that he could be so cold-blooded about everything, not with all she now knew him capable of, but it still came as an unpleasant shock to hear anyone discuss killing another person with such an utter lack of feeling. The man truly was insane.

"Now," he said. "Enough talk. Let's go. I haven't got all night."

She and Matt exchanged a glance, clearly having reached the same conclusion. They'd exhausted all their arguments for the time being, and Walt had swatted them away one by one as though they were nothing. There didn't seem to be anything they could do at the moment but comply.

Walt had them walk straight out behind the house and into the pasture beyond. They moved in silence.

Elena spotted the truck long before they arrived at it, the vehicle slowly growing larger as they approached. Her dread grew with every step, her desperation for a plan—any plan—that could get them out of this rising with each second. What would happen when they got there? Would he no longer need Matt to be alive and capable of walking?

No, she realized. She shouldn't have underestimated Walt's laziness. If he killed Matt here, he still would have to get him back out of the truck and carry him to wherever he intended to dispose of his body. His plan required Matt to disappear, seemingly with her. No trace of his body could be found. They had some time.

Just not very much.

They finally made it to the truck. Matt and Elena stopped behind the vehicle and glanced back at him.

Walt was frowning. He eyed the truckbed, then the two of them. She could see his mind working, watched him try to figure out what to do. Elena considered their own options, her thoughts likely leading her to the same place his were. He couldn't have a very steady grip on his weapon while he was driving. If one of them was in the front with him, they could try to make a move, go for the gun or the wheel. If it was her, he'd be more hesitant to shoot, not wanting to kill her, not before he could do what he wanted with her. If it was Matt, he would be even stronger, have more of a chance to fight back. And if one of them was in the back, they could try to jump out and make a run for it. Or better yet, they could hop out the side and try to get into the driver's side to him and the gun.

They were all good possibilities—for them, offering at least a chance. So she wasn't surprised when he didn't go with any of them.

Walt reached into his pocket with his free hand and pulled out his keys. He tossed them at Elena's feet. "You're driving. Alvarez, you're in the middle, and I'm riding shotgun." His lips curled back, revealing a lot of teeth. "Literally. I'm going to have my gun in your side the whole time. Elena, you try anything funny behind the wheel, and I pull the trigger. Alvarez, you try making a move, same result. Got it?"

Elena swallowed hard, her heart plummeting. Walt might be lazy and deranged, but he wasn't completely stupid. It was the best scenario—for him at least, keeping them both firmly under control.

Walt was still waiting for an answer. There was just one problem with his plan. She raised her bound wrists. "How am I supposed to drive with these on?"

He eyed her for a long moment, as though wondering if she was trying to pull something. Or maybe he just wasn't happy about having a big flaw in his plan pointed out.

In one swift motion he reached down to his belt, unhooked one key from a loop and tossed it onto the ground in front of her with the keys to the truck. "There," he said. "Unlock the cuffs, but don't even think of trying anything."

Elena made herself nod, unable to squelch a tiny sense of triumph. It would be much more possible to do something with her hands free. What that would be, she didn't know. It wasn't much, but it was a start.

"Okay," he said. "Let's get going."

He motioned to the keys, and Elena slowly bent to retrieve them. When she had the handcuffs off, she tossed them back to him on the ground in front of him, then reached for the keys to the truck. Once she had them in hand, Walt gestured for her to go to the driver's side, Matt to head to the passenger's. Once they'd done as ordered, Walt fell into step behind Matt, keeping his gun aimed at his back.

With numb fingers Elena opened the door. She was about to climb inside when the passenger door opened, Matt standing on the other side. Their eyes met across the length of the cab. He gave a barely perceptible nod, his gaze narrowed and hard, his expression resolute. It was a signal to her, an indication he had a plan and everything was going to be all right.

And she knew, her heart stopping dead in her chest. He was going to try something. He was going to make a move or go for the gun or…something. Something reckless and stupid that would put him in danger, all with the intention of trying to save her.

Staring at him in shock, she almost shook her head. She didn't want him risking his life for her, damn well didn't want him *sacrificing* it.

Even if she'd been foolish enough to try to communicate a message to him, she didn't get a chance. He ducked his head and climbed into the cab, sliding across the seat to the middle. Walt followed quickly behind.

Elena had no choice but to get in, too. She landed right beside Matt, their thighs and arms squeezed tightly together. The feel of him there offered no comfort, only reminding her of how much danger he was in.

Closing the door, she slowly stuck the key in the ignition and started the engine. "Where are we going?" Elena asked, trying to keep her voice steady.

"I'll let you know. Just head straight."

She did as he said, shifting the vehicle into Drive and pressing down on the gas, sending the truck straight on into the night.

They drove across the back pasture, out into the heart of the spread. Elena might not know exactly where he was taking them, but she could imagine too well. The back acreage offered access to a vast number of isolated spots—both on the property and beyond—where no one would notice them heading, and where Matt could disappear with little hope of being discovered for a very long time, if ever. And then Walt would have her all to himself.

She continued to go through every available option. There had to be something, anything, she could do.

If she slammed on the brakes, Walt could be startled into pulling the trigger. All that would result in was Matt being shot. She wouldn't be able to do anything, not for him, not to Walt with an injured Matt between them.

If she suddenly swerved in either direction, same result. Walt startled into firing, Matt shot, her helpless. No good.

What if—

Matt bumped his knee into hers twice, the action deliberate enough to let her know it was no accident.

She tried not to betray a single reaction, giving no indication she'd noticed the gesture.

Out of the corner of her eye, she saw him tilt his head slightly to the left. A few seconds later he repeated the motion, again leaving her no doubt it was no accident.

She glanced down. He made a tiny, downward motion with his hand.

Nothing else immediately followed, leaving her pondering the meaning behind his cues.

Something…left and down. What could that mean? Obviously he wanted her to do something.

He bumped her with his elbow, nudging her toward the door.

Left. Down. Door.

No.

She couldn't be reading him correctly. He couldn't possibly want her to do what she thought he did.

Because if she was correct, he wanted her to jump out of the truck.

Under different circumstances, she might have gawked at him. If that was what he wanted her to do, then he was out of his mind. What good could that do? She wasn't concerned about her own safety. Falling out of a moving vehicle would hurt, but at this speed, she would be fine. And if it would save him, she would do it. But if she threw the door open and suddenly fell out, he would immediately shoot Matt.

Or would he?

Jumping out of the truck wouldn't jostle him the way hitting the brakes or swerving would. It would surprise him, but not in the same way. It would take him a second to understand what was happening, to react to it. Which meant he likely wouldn't pull the trigger right away. No, there would be that split-second delay, which Matt might be able to use to his advantage to do…something.

Maybe. He still had his hands fastened behind his back after all.

It was a big hurdle, possibly an insurmountable one. Frankly, she couldn't see how he'd overcome it—

Matt nudged her again with his elbow. Harder this time. Insistent.

She wanted to nudge him back—hard—but was afraid Walt would notice. They were lucky he hadn't called them on any of these signals yet.

She had to trust he was right on this. And she did, to a degree. She trusted he believed this would save her. She just didn't trust he intended for it to do the same for him.

It couldn't happen. She couldn't lose him. They hadn't come this far, found each other again after so long, only for her to lose him now.

Still, she couldn't delay forever. They had every reason to believe that Matt was already living on borrowed time. Walt could very well intend their destination, wherever it was, to serve as Matt's final resting place. She saw the way Walt kept leaning forward slightly and glancing over at her. He couldn't keep his eyes off her. How had she never noticed how creepy the way he looked at her was? Whether he'd managed to hide it better before, he wasn't now. He wanted her alone, to have her all to himself. Which meant Matt's time was running out.

No, wherever they were going, she had to act before they got there.

She had to do this.

She quickly went through everything she had to do. It was simple really. Grab the doorknob. Open the door. Fall out. Whatever Matt had planned, that would be the tricky part.

She could do this. She *had* to do this.

She braced herself against the door.

It happened in seconds, faster than she'd imagined.

She grabbed the handle.

The door popped open.

She tumbled out, her leg slamming against the door as she went.

She barely noticed it, because it seemed that almost instantly she hit the ground, the landing jarring every bone in her body. Weeds and shrubs hit her, scratched her, as she rolled over and over, dirt filling her nose and eyes.

She finally managed to slow her momentum, until she flopped over onto her back and landed. Coughing, blinking to clear her vision, she immediately pushed herself up, ignoring the aches and pains in her bones and hand, seeking out the truck.

Then she saw it, still rumbling along, but gradually slowing, the driver's-side door hanging open. It was too far away for her to make out what was happening in the cab.

Elena pushed herself all the way to her feet, preparing to break into a run. She had to try to help Matt. She couldn't let Walt hurt him.

A gunshot rang out.

She'd just begun moving. Instead, she stumbled to a stop, her whole body tensing in horror.

No.

It couldn't be. Matt had somehow managed to get the gun away. Nothing else was possible. He couldn't have been shot. He couldn't be hurt or bleeding or gone….

Her legs nearly gave way and she almost fell to her knees.

Her vision began to burn again, harder this time, no longer from the dust, but from the sheer agony gripping her body, squeezing her heart, compressing her lungs.

She remembered this feeling. It felt as if she was dying.

The way she'd felt the first time she'd lost him.

The seconds ticked by. She needed to move. She needed to go and see.

But somehow, no matter how hard she tried, she couldn't compel her body to move. Because if something had happened to him, she couldn't face it, not losing him, not forever.

Once again she wouldn't have gotten to say goodbye.

The truck continued to roll forward, still slowing gradually, its progress across the flat earth eerie in the moonlight.

Suddenly, as though hitting an invisible wall, it slammed to a halt.

She waited. If Walt stepped out of the truck, she would need to run. Even if she hardly felt the need to fight anymore.

Then she heard it.

"Elena!"

She recognized the voice immediately.

Matt. It was Matt.

The air wheezed from her lungs.

He didn't sound hurt. He sounded fine. He sounded safe.

She lunged into motion, running the rest of the way to the truck as fast and as hard as her legs could carry her, stumbling and lurching the whole way.

Then she was there, at the still-open driver's-side door.

And found herself staring at Matt's back and cuffed wrists.

She gaped in disbelief, not understanding what she was seeing.

He sat in the driver's seat, his back to the open doorway. She peered over his shoulder. Walt was slumped in his seat, his chin to his chest, clearly unconscious.

"How did you—"

Matt glanced back at her, meeting her eyes. "Go around the other side and get the keys to the cuffs," he said. "I need you to unfasten mine and get a pair on this bastard before he wakes up."

She wasted no time doing exactly that, hurrying around the front of the truck to the passenger side. Walt's arm and shoulder were against the door, so she opened it slowly, careful not to jar him or let him fall out. When she had the door open, she leaned in and over him. She spotted the keys looped to Walt's belt, along with another pair of cuffs, maybe the ones she'd taken off. Grabbing the cuffs, she fastened them on Walt's wrists—extra tight, just the way he liked them. Without bothering to close the door, she took the keys and raced back to the other side.

As soon as she was there, Matt shifted to allow her easy access to the cuffs. She had them open in ten seconds flat.

Then he was shifting in the seat, sliding out of the cab, stepping onto the ground and forward to catch her in his arms.

Elena threw her arms around him, sagging against him.

"I don't understand. How did you do it?"

"My hands were bound, so I had to use my feet. As soon as you opened the door and I saw his head turn, I twisted and slid over onto the driver's side and started kicking, going for the gun first, then his head."

She gaped at him in horror. "He could have shot you."

"But he didn't."

"You're out of your mind."

"It worked, didn't it?"

"You're lucky it did."

"I was thinking earlier we were due a little luck, weren't we?"

As she looked into the humor laughing in his eyes, she couldn't help it. A laugh escaped her lips, too. "I guess you're right."

Yes, she thought, after everything they'd been through in the past few days, it had been time for something to go their way. And it had. It hardly seemed possible, but they'd made it. They'd won. They were still standing.

Together.

Chapter Sixteen

Elena stood on the back porch and stared out into the night. It was a clear, warm evening. A multitude of stars glittered in the inky-black sky, and the moon cast its glow upon the land that stretched before her as far as the eye could see. Weston land. Her land now, though not for long. She'd wanted to leave here for so long. The ranch had been connected with so much unhappiness for her—more than she'd even known—but she couldn't deny the beauty of the land.

It was a lovely night. Peaceful. So peaceful that it was almost impossible to believe the ranch had been the scene of so much activity and turmoil in the past few days.

In the wake of Walt's attack, Matt had wasted no time contacting his friend Pam with the FBI, wanting someone on their side as they dealt with the aftermath. With a deputy dead and the sheriff responsible, they knew they were going to need all the help they could find to get anyone to believe their story and take their word over his. Pam had made the initial contact with the state authorities, who had quickly descended on the scene. Pam had arrived soon afterward with several of her own colleagues, the Bureau's standing investigation into the missing women and possible serial killer giving them some claim for jurisdiction in the case.

As expected, the state authorities had initially been hesitant to believe Matt and Elena over Walt, with his long history in law enforcement. But there was too much about the circumstances of that night that didn't line up with his version of events, like why Matt and Elena would have driven off with him instead of killing him like Travis if they were the killers. A search of his home turned up additional evidence that Walt had been involved in Big Jim's murderous activities—and had continued on his own in the years since. It seemed Big Jim wasn't the only one who liked to keep souvenirs close at hand.

It hadn't taken the crime scene investigators long to find where Big Jim had buried the bodies of his and Walt's victims on the ranch property. Elena had been there when the remaining bones had started to be uncovered. It would be some time before the bodies were accurately identified, if they ever could be, and there was no way of knowing yet whether Teresa Reyes was among them. Elena was aware of that. She hadn't cared. After all the times she'd hated her mother for leaving them, blamed her for what her father had become, wondered how she could have abandoned her child, she'd needed to be there. So when the first bones began to emerge, she'd been there to witness it, tears in her eyes, trying to hold back the sobs, until they'd finally broken free and Matt had taken her in his arms and held her while she wept.

He'd been by her side that day, and every day since that night, her only constant in a world that seemed to have turned upside down on her. She didn't know what she would have done without him. She hoped to never have to experience that again.

Even as she thought it, she heard the screen door behind her squeal softly as it was opened. She didn't have to look to see who it was. Even if there was anyone else it could have been, she had no trouble recognizing him, her body instantly responding to his nearness, attuned to his presence on a molecular level that was undeniable.

He didn't say anything as he came up behind her and wrapped his arms around her waist. She leaned back against him, resting her head on his shoulder, sinking into the sensations of his body and his touch as her eyes drifted shut.

"Hey," he murmured against her hair. "You okay?"

"Yeah," she whispered back. "Just thinking."

"Having second thoughts?"

"No." The land might be beautiful, but more than ever she knew she couldn't stay here. Selling was the right thing to do.

In the midst of everything that had happened, she hadn't had a chance to contact Glen until tonight to see if his offer still stood. He'd admitted that he hadn't been certain he still wanted to buy the ranch, now that he knew the truth about Big Jim. Elena had guessed as much when he hadn't tried to contact her himself sooner. She wouldn't have blamed him for taking back his offer, though she would have been disappointed. It was only natural that the property would be tainted in a lot of people's minds due to what had happened here. If Glen no longer wanted it, it could take her a long time to find another buyer.

Fortunately, Glen had decided to continue with the

sale. Big Jim may not have been the man he'd believed him to be, but that didn't change the work generations of Westons had put into the land. Junior and Bobby had still been his friends, practically his sons, and for their sake, he would go forth with his original plan to try to maintain the property, the way they would have wanted.

And she had a feeling he would have a much better time of it. Matt had told her about Jack's belief that the place had bad vibes. Elena wasn't sure she believed in that, but she had to admit that in the days since the bodies had been removed from the property, the ranch felt different. Happier.

"And you're really sure about letting this place go?"

She nodded. "I'm sure." Even if the ranch wasn't connected with so much unhappiness for her, Bobby had given his heart and soul to running it and he hadn't been able to make it work. There was little chance she could succeed where he'd failed, especially when she wasn't nearly as invested. Glen would have a much better chance of doing something worthwhile with the ranch than she ever could. "It's the right thing to do. And the amount of money Glen's offering should be enough to pay off the remaining debts here, with enough left over for me to start over somewhere else."

"Where do you want to go?" he asked softly.

It was a very good question. "I'm not sure," she admitted. "I haven't really had a chance to think about it."

She just knew she needed to get away from Western Bluff. The past few days had made that clear enough. No one had apologized for their suspicions or the way they'd acted toward her. If anything, things were just as tense and uncomfortable as they'd been immediately after Bobby's murder. A lot of people were still avoiding her or looked away when they saw her in town, but now it was more out of embarrassment than distrust.

The only exception had been Lynda Clayton. After the news had gotten out about the true fate of Elena's mother, Lynda had arrived on her doorstep, tears in her eyes.

"Does Henry know you're here?" Elena had been unable to keep from asking.

"I don't know, and I don't care," she'd said without hesitation.

Her tone was honest enough Elena hadn't doubted she meant it. Still, she hadn't known quite what to do as Lynda had stared at her, her eyes poring over Elena's face with unnerving scrutiny, the tears coming harder.

"You look like her," Lynda had finally whispered.

The wrenching pain in her voice had cracked something open in Elena and suddenly she'd been crying, too. She'd barely known how to begin grieving for her mother, a woman who'd been gone most of her life and whom she hardly remembered. But seeing Lynda's profound anguish had somehow released Elena's own sorrow. This woman she barely knew, who'd brought Matt back into her life, was the only person grieving her mother, too, who cared about her as a person. Even more, she was the only one who could tell her about Teresa. Her tears flowing freely, Elena had automatically opened her arms, and Lynda had fallen into them. They'd clung together for a while before going inside for a long talk. Lynda had shared just a fraction of her memories, and for the first time Elena had been able to learn about who Teresa had been. Not just the abstract idea of a mother who hadn't been there, but the real flesh-and-blood woman she was. They'd talked for hours, and Elena knew that wherever she went, her newfound relationship with Lynda was one connection to the town she would keep.

It was likely to be the only one. Once the ranch was sold there would be nothing keeping her here. She could go practically anywhere. She had a college degree she'd never used. She could start a career like she'd always dreamed of, doing almost anything she wanted. The vast number of possibilities that lay before her were overwhelming.

This was what she'd wanted practically her entire life, to get away from this town. And now that the moment was finally here and the whole world was available to her, she didn't know where she wanted to go.

There was only one thing she did know: wherever she went, she wanted it to be with Matt.

She opened her mouth to say just that when he reached over and turned her to face him.

She peered up into his eyes, her heart leaping into her throat at the sight of him and the intensity in his gaze.

"Come with me."

Past and present merged in front of her. She'd lived this moment before. Yet here it was again, a second chance she'd never dreamed possible.

"Where?" she asked, suddenly breathless.

"Wherever I go."

"Back to New Mexico?"

He hesitated, then lifted one shoulder in a helpless little shrug. "To start. I want you to meet everybody there. But maybe not forever. Like I told you, I don't know if I want to work on the Triple C the rest of my life, not to mention I can't imagine there being enough for you to do there. Maybe I want my own place. Maybe I should try something new. I don't know where I'm going any more than you do. But I know I want you with me. If you'll have me."

It was exactly what he'd offered her before, exactly what she'd feared the most. A life of uncertainty. It wasn't what she'd dreamed of, it wasn't what she'd ever wanted for her life.

But this time she wasn't afraid. How could she be? After everything they'd been through, everything they'd overcome, she couldn't imagine anything that they couldn't deal with together. And second chances were so rare in this life. She wasn't about to let this one get away.

"Yes," she said, happiness soaring through her. The feeling only grew, surging higher and fiercer as she watched the smile dawn on his face, the sheer joy in his eyes.

He lunged forward and caught her in his arms, lifting her straight off her feet and pulling her tight against him.

Laughing, Elena held on to him just as tightly, never wanting to let go, knowing she never would. The future lay before them, vast and unknown, not scary, but thrilling.

Because they didn't need certainty. They didn't need a plan.

They needed only love. And each other.

They had that.

And she couldn't wait to discover the beautiful future they'd find together.

* * * * *

REQUEST YOUR FREE BOOKS!
2 FREE NOVELS PLUS 2 FREE GIFTS!

❦ Harlequin®
INTRIGUE®
BREATHTAKING ROMANTIC SUSPENSE

YES! Please send me 2 FREE Harlequin Intrigue® novels and my 2 FREE gifts (gifts are worth about $10). After receiving them, if I don't wish to receive any more books, I can return the shipping statement marked "cancel." If I don't cancel, I will receive 6 brand-new novels every month and be billed just $4.49 per book in the U.S. or $5.24 per book in Canada. That's a saving of at least 14% off the cover price! It's quite a bargain! Shipping and handling is just 50¢ per book in the U.S. and 75¢ per book in Canada.* I understand that accepting the 2 free books and gifts places me under no obligation to buy anything. I can always return a shipment and cancel at any time. Even if I never buy another book, the two free books and gifts are mine to keep forever.

182/382 HDN FEQ2

Name		
	(PLEASE PRINT)	

Address		Apt. #

City	State/Prov.	Zip/Postal Code

Signature (if under 18, a parent or guardian must sign)

Mail to the **Reader Service:**
IN U.S.A.: P.O. Box 1867, Buffalo, NY 14240-1867
IN CANADA: P.O. Box 609, Fort Erie, Ontario L2A 5X3

Not valid for current subscribers to Harlequin Intrigue books.

**Are you a subscriber to Harlequin Intrigue books
and want to receive the larger-print edition?
Call 1-800-873-8635 or visit www.ReaderService.com.**

* Terms and prices subject to change without notice. Prices do not include applicable taxes. Sales tax applicable in N.Y. Canadian residents will be charged applicable taxes. Offer not valid in Quebec. This offer is limited to one order per household. All orders subject to credit approval. Credit or debit balances in a customer's account(s) may be offset by any other outstanding balance owed by or to the customer. Please allow 4 to 6 weeks for delivery. Offer available while quantities last.

Your Privacy—The Reader Service is committed to protecting your privacy. Our Privacy Policy is available online at www.ReaderService.com or upon request from the Reader Service.

We make a portion of our mailing list available to reputable third parties that offer products we believe may interest you. If you prefer that we not exchange your name with third parties, or if you wish to clarify or modify your communication preferences, please visit us at www.ReaderService.com/consumerschoice or write to us at Reader Service Preference Service, P.O. Box 9062, Buffalo, NY 14269. Include your complete name and address.

HI11B

HARLEQUIN®

SYTYCW
SO YOU THINK YOU CAN WRITE

Harlequin and Mills & Boon are joining forces in a global search for new authors.

In September 2012 we're launching our biggest contest yet—with the prize of being published by the world's leader in romance fiction!

Look for more information on our website,
www.soyouthinkyoucanwrite.com

So you think you can write? Show us!

*In the newest continuity series from Harlequin®
Romantic Suspense, the worlds of the Coltons and their
Amish neighbors collide—with dramatic results.*

*Take a sneak peek at the first book, COLTON DESTINY
by Justine Davis, available September 2012.*

"**I**'m here to try and find your sister."

"I know this. But don't assume this will automatically ensure trust from all of us."

He was antagonizing her. Purposely.

Caleb realized it with a little jolt. While it was difficult for anyone in the community to turn to outsiders for help, they had all reluctantly agreed this was beyond their scope and that they would cooperate.

Including—in fact, especially—him.

"Then I will find these girls without your help," she said, sounding fierce.

Caleb appreciated her determination. He *wanted* that kind of determination in the search for Hannah. He attempted a fresh start.

"It is difficult for us—"

"What's difficult for me is to understand why anyone wouldn't pull out all the stops to save a child whose life could be in danger."

Caleb wasn't used to being interrupted. Annie would never have dreamed of it. But this woman was clearly nothing like his sweet, retiring Annie. She was sharp, forceful and very intense.

"I grew up just a couple of miles from here," she said. "And I always had the idea the Amish loved their kids just as we did."

"Of course we do."

"And yet you'll throw roadblocks in the way of the people best equipped to find your missing children?"

Caleb studied her for a long, silent moment. "You are very angry," he said.

"Of course I am."

"Anger is an...unproductive emotion."

She stared at him in turn then. "Oh, it can be very productive. Perhaps you could use a little."

"It is not our way."

"Is it your way to stand here and argue with me when your sister is among the missing?"

Caleb gave himself an internal shake. Despite her abrasiveness—well, when compared to Annie, anyway—he could not argue with her last point. And he wasn't at all sure why he'd found himself sparring with this woman. She was an Englishwoman, and what they said or did mattered nothing to him.

Except it had to matter now. For Hannah's sake.

Don't miss any of the books in this exciting new miniseries from Harlequin® Romantic Suspense, starting in September 2012 and running through December 2012.